Fisherman's Beach

Fisherman's Beach

GEORGE VUKELICH

NORTH COUNTRY PRESS

Published 1990

North Country Press
3934 Plymouth Circle
Madison, WI 53705

First North Country Press printing
Originally published in 1962 by St. Martin's Press, New York

Printed in the United States of America
Cover designed by Jane Tenenbaum

Library of Congress Catalog Card Number 62-16183
ISBN 0-944133-08-8

for Mari Sandoz

Fisherman's Beach

1

It was the last of March when the big breakup began. The ice field cracked like cannon shots and the white surface creviced like plate glass and the hot sun and the high winds swept the shores of the great inland sea like herring gulls hunting out small fish. Then one morning in the middle of April the black, soggy pack ice and the scum ice were gone and Lake Michigan burst free, rolling and slashing like a sturgeon fish tearing out of the pot net and springtime came to the fisherman's beach.

Over the stretch of Wisconsin shore owned by Old Man LeMere, patches of the old snow clung like scabs. The stink of creosote rose on the east wind as the Old Man's sons began to tar the miles and miles of nets and spread them out on the sand dunes. The nets would set and harden stiff as steel cable before they were strung out on the spiles that would anchor them in the fishing grounds until the cold weather of autumn came again.

The high winds confined all the work to the beach. With the hard sea running they could not begin the work of spile driving and setting the nets. The sons of Old LeMere worked among the soiled patches of melting snow and waited for the weather to be good.

From his bedroom the Old Man watched the work. He cursed the strong spring winds that confined his sons to the beach and he cursed Coutre who had confined him to this prison of a bedroom.

"That horse doctor has put me in hell," he said.

Reuben looked up from his book on the floor. His green eyes widened under the thick shock of black hair.

"What horse doctor, Papa?"

The Old Man stared at his youngest son. Was there a smile playing hide-and-seek in that innocent ten-year-old face?

"That damned Coutre," the Old Man bellowed.

"I didn't know he doctored horses," Reuben said.

"Horses. Dogs. Cats." The Old Man roared in his frustration. "Coutre is an excellent doctor for dumb animals." The sight of the huge unlaunched spile driver on the beach angered him and the feel of his nightshirt angered him and he cracked his knobby knuckles and punched his scarred fists into his palms.

Jesus Lord Christ! At the time he was needed most Coutre put him on the beach like an old hull with the dry rot. And not only Coutre. Mama too. Leave it to Mama. He looked out at the wild unleashed waters smashing into the beachlands.

5

It comes to everyone, LeMere knew. Year after year after year, there was no holding nature. It worked at eroding a man. Gnawing. Nibbling. Smashing. Grinding. Working on him. Trying to pry him apart in the very same way that a clam is forced apart. And then one day, after the beatings and the poundings, and the erosion, a man realized that there was no holding nature. A man gave up and there it was—death—inside his shell, his body, sucking out the heart of him. LeMere ran a hand through his full white mane. And there was no defense. A man aged . . . a man aged.

"Reuben," the Old Man said softly, "do you know what your dear good mother has done with the bottle?"

"The brandy, sir?"

"The brandy, indeed."

Reuben hesitated.

"Yes, sir. I know what Mama has done with the bottle."

Slowly, the Old Man drew up his knees and hunched forward on his folded arms; he looked like a sea gull sitting on a spile top.

"Reuben, while I realize that your Irish mother has endowed you with a remarkably cold streak of practicality, may I remind you that you have inherited from your French father a certain measure of the milk of human kindness. Now, fetch the bottle."

Uncertainly Reuben closed *Treasure Island* and got to his feet.

"Is it for a medicinal purpose, Papa?"

The Old Man sighed and touched his heart.

"Oh, the pains are bad, Reuben. I may be going this time. Indeed, the purpose is medicinal." He coughed a racking cough and bulged his eyes.

A frightened look crossed Reuben's face like a wind shift over a sand bar and then he dropped the book and bolted through the bedroom door.

"And a large glass of water," the Old Man yelled after him. Old LeMere rubbed the white stubble of his beard and then looked down and patted his heart.

"Now then, for the sake of a dishonest old gull, please do not stop before he gets back with the bottle," he said.

The Old Man watched through the window. It was reassuring to see his sons throwing their shoulders into the work—stretching the endless nets. They moved about the beach tasks as men who knew what they were about. Roger and the twins, Raphael and Gabriel. Each of them standing over six feet in his booted feet and built from the ground up like ax handles. Yes, he had given his boys strength and that strength linked his sons together like the links of an anchor chain. He, LeMere, had given his sons the bodies of bulls. Their mother had given them the laughter of the Irish. Indeed, the French and the Irish had produced a good working breed for this fisherman's beach. Three sons who were fine fisherman. Roger, Raphael, and Gabriel. Three sons who would soon be joined by young Reuben and then there would be four. Four sons. God had truly been good to him. What more could an Old Man ask? Four sons straight as spiles and strong as the steel cable. And then the Old Man thought of the fifth son. The oldest son. The prodigal son. The Old Man thought of Germaine.

"Are you all right, Papa?"

Reuben was back with the bottle and watching him closely. The Old Man smiled at the boy.

"You are a good son, Reuben, I should not play tricks on you."

Reuben handed him the bottle.

"I thought it was a trick, sir."

The Old Man uncapped the brandy and tilted the bottle.

"So, then, and why did you think it was a trick?"

"Because, sir, when you had the real pains you tried to hide them; this time you weren't trying to hide them at all. Anyway, I don't think you drink too much, sir!"

"Bless you, Reuben. A finer diagnosis of my case I have never heard."

He closed his eyes and tilted the bottle again.

The front door slammed and the Old Man opened his eyes and lowered the bottle. He listened carefully.

"That sounds like Mama. Reuben, look and see if the truck is back."

"Yes, sir," he said excitedly, "the truck is back."

The Old Man was corking up the bottle hurriedly and the brandy sloshed and some of it spilled onto the patch quilt. He dabbed at the spreading wet stain and held the bottle out to Reuben.

"Under the bed with it, boy. Quickly, or we are trapped like fish in a net."

Reuben was on his knees shoving the bottle under the bed when his mother's voice floated into the bedroom.

"Bébé, come into the kitchen."

The boy scrambled to his feet brushing the knees of his bluejeans and stared down at the opening. Then without hesitation he pulled the bedspread loose so that it draped onto the floor.

"I'll have to set the table for dinner," he said. His voice dropped to a whisper. "Do you think it will be all right under the bed?"

"Indeed, you have done valiant work this day, Reuben," the Old Man whispered. "We shall guard *it* with our very lives."

Mama called again and Reuben ran from the room.

The Old Man rubbed his palm over the place where the brandy had spilled. He put his hand to his nose, sniffed, licked his fingers and his lips. The old age was into his flesh like a gaff hook, his excitements were not many these days. He stiffened the pillows behind his back, folded his hands, and looked out the window.

His boys would be having their dinner soon. Good meat and potatoes and bread and second and third helpings all the way around and then one of Mama's homemade pies and coffee and cigarettes and time for a little talk over a bottle of beer or two. The Old Man sighed and thought sadly of his little bowl of broth and knew that hell must be like this.

Reuben appeared in the doorway. Over his dark blue sweater he had one of Mama's aprons snugged under his armpits. He looked a little bit afraid.

"Father Doucette," he said. "He's here to see you, Papa. He rode back from town in the truck with Mama." The old priest was behind the boy now, his two hundred pounds filling the doorway. "He's staying for dinner, too," Reuben said weakly. He nodded up at the priest's red face and to his father. Then he fled.

Father Doucette walked into the room with the roll of a man once given to ship decks in the rolling inland seas.

Doucette, the Old Man thought, chugged around like a little fish tug full right up to the gunwales.

"I heard from Coutre about your heart," he said. "He painted a very bad picture so I came to see for myself."

"That damned Coutre is part undertaker," the Old Man said. "Have a seat, Father."

"Agreed," the priest said, settling himself by the bed. He scratched his bald spot in mock perplexity. "I must admit that when I saw Mama in town I did not know whether to come out and give you the Last Rites or help her price a casket." The priest dug in the pocket of his leather jacket for cigarettes. "Aaaah, that Coutre. He has half my parish dead and buried already. A very pessimistic man."

The priest lighted a cigarette and drew deeply. He put the dead match in his black trouser cuff. The laughter left his large blue eyes.

"Man to man now," he said, straight at the Old Man, "how goes it?"

"How goes it? What the hell, Father. A little rest and I will be as good as new. I am not the kind of man to die in bed."

"Coutre is worried about you," the priest said. "We are all worried."

The Old Man looked away from the priest and shrugged his shoulders.

"God's will, Father."

The priest smiled, the crow's-feet spread above the big honest nose.

"Now you are talking *my* language." He drew on the cigarette, his white brows drooping like wings. "Agreed, it is God's will that we all die but not that we kill ourselves."

He tapped the cigarette ash into his cuff. "Coutre thinks that you should give up this fishing. I think so too."

The Old Man looked out the window at the broad backs of his sons bending into their work. How many years had it been? How many seasons of working the fish grounds as the farmer works his fields. Ten. Twenty. Thirty. Forty. The years packed away in the fish boxes like the gutted trout, gills and all. A fisherman measures out his life by the storms he has seen, the pot nets he has lifted, the oil drums of fish offal, and the sons he has raised—the sons who would inherit the nets and spiles and the boats and the barges and the buildings and a way of life. The sons who would come to own the old fisherman's beach. How many years to make it so?

The Old Man moved a hand to his face. The soft green eyes were moist.

"I am sorry, Father. I was thinking."

The old priest wrinkled his nose and sniffed like an old birddog testing the wind.

"God save us all," he said, "why start now?"

He stared at the bedspread hanging nearly to the floor like a tent flap and he smiled.

"Well, if I smell what I think I smell, let us do some thinking together."

The Old Man's face lighted slowly; he pointed under the bed.

"Sssh," he said, putting his forefinger to his lips. "We will be violating a local ordinance."

The priest got down on all fours and raised the bedspread and crawled forward a little. The Old Man looked down at the wide expanse of Father Doucette's bottom wedged under the bedsprings and shook his head. The priest backed out slowly.

"You don't leave a man much head room," he said.

"I was thinking," the Old Man said, "if you had been in bed and I was getting the bottle, we would both die of thirst."

The priest sat down on the floor and laughed and opened the bottle. He held it out to the Old Man.

"No, you first, Father. You are my guest."

The priest wiped the bottle top; he drank and blew through his lips and passed the bottle up to the bed.

"Coutre told you to stop the drinking?"

The Old Man wiped the bottle and nodded.

"He must think you are very sick."

The Old Man swallowed quickly and then once more.

"Sick! Coutre must think I am dead!"

He passed the bottle back. The priest raised himself and backed up to the chair and sprawled into it.

"So," he said, "how goes it?"

The Old Man smiled. The liquor was warming him and he felt good.

"Good," he said.

"You know," the priest said, "you have a little money. You can retire and go somewhere with Mama. Coutre thinks the Southwest. He goes himself every winter."

"I am not as sick as Coutre."

"Your boys are all men now. They can work the beach and you can take Reuben with you."

The Old Man sat very still for a long time.

"Father, I'll tell you. My sons, Roger and the twins, Raphael and Gabriel—and I do not include Reuben because he is not yet a grown man—my sons are all grown men and as you say they can work the beach. They have the youth and they are strong as I once was. But, Father, this fishing is a business full of responsibilities and worries like the lake is full of weeds."

The Old Man stopped and stared at the priest.

"I am not saying it well. They are all stronger than I was. Smarter, too, I do not know. They are just young yet, Father. Their heads are full of the women, anybody's women, as you well know from your confessional. They are not settled yet. I have to hold my sons together until one of them is ready. Roger wants to take my place, but he is too hotheaded, too stubborn. He would have everybody pulling every which way. He is worried too much about Roger and not enough about his brothers. But then young men are like that. When they get it beaten out of them, we shall see."

The Old Man sighed.

"I do not know, Father. They have a passion for the money I pay them. But they are young. Perhaps they will come to love this great water when they are older."

"Perhaps," the priest said. "Perhaps yes. Perhaps no."

"I tell you the truth, Father. A man must love his work like he loves his woman." He looked at the priest's Roman collar peeking out under his chins. "Or his God, Father. When one of my sons comes to love fishing that way . . ." The Old Man's voice trailed away like a track of foam, "to that son will I give this Fisherman's Beach."

The priest lowered his eyes and pulled at his nose.

The Old Man's voice came slow and steady like a breaker rolling onto the shore.

"These are hard days, Father. Already, last season the

trout were not so plentiful. If it goes like that this year and perhaps worse . . ." the Old Man shrugged. "Someone has to run things. Someone has to hold them together."

They sat looking at each other for a long time. The only sound in the room was the wind outside gnawing at the frame house, the wind and the Lake Michigan surf forty yards beyond the front door pounding onto the beach.

"Old Coutre is right, Father. But what's to be done? Better to die in my boots all at once than in little pieces in some strange hotel."

The priest nodded and smiled and raised the bottle.

"That makes something," he said. "Yes . . . may God be with you always, my friend. May he bless your boys also and this beach." He drank and handed the bottle to the Old Man.

Downstairs the dinner bell rang on the winter porch. The wind carried it across the dune sand and into the dark pine firs where the Point Beach forest stretched for miles and miles.

"I am not the kind to die in bed," the Old Man said. He swallowed quickly. Then he raised the bottle to his lips and drank slowly . . . deliberately.

When he was finished, Father Doucette put the bottle back under the bed. Mama came up with the broth for the Old Man and the priest went down to wash up for dinner.

"He looks good," the priest told Mama as he was leaving. "He is a tough old gull."

By the wall clock in the rectory of Saint Luke's, it was ten o'clock that evening before Father Doucette was finished with the letter that Mama LeMere had given him. He had read the words she had written and added a full page of his own. Then Doctor Coutre had lighted his pipe and read the letter earnestly . . . grunting. As he bent to scrawl a note of his own, he looked like some sort of tall ungainly bird, jammed into a small nest. A blue heron, the priest thought. An old one.

Father Doucette clucked at his friend.

"It is a bad hand you write for an educated man, Coutre. This looks something like a prescription."

Coutre rapped out his pipe ash and put the briar in his pocket.

"Well, Joe," he said, "I'll tell you. It is something of a prescription. Now seal the thing up and I'll mail it on the way home."

Coutre had written a long paragraph. The last sentence said simply: "Because of his general deterioration—and for your Mother's sake—I, too, suggest your immediate return, if at all humanly possible."

Father Doucette licked the glue flap and pressed the envelope down on the green desk blotter. He found an Air Mail sticker and pasted that on too.

"This glue would drive a man to drink," he said.

"Well, one little one for the road then?" Coutre asked. He refilled the two glasses.

Father Doucette stared down at the white face of the envelope. He had typed the address himself.

Major Germaine LeMere
1408 Base Unit AAF
APO 741
N.Y., N.Y.

The priest took off his horn rims and the address blurred into fuzzy black lines.

The eyes are the windows of the soul. It was funny how that saying he had learned as a child always came back to him when he took the glasses away from his nearsighted eyes. Father Doucette sighed and reminded himself to have the keys of his old typewriter cleaned one of these days. Then he reached out carefully for his drink.

"I don't like to see him looking like that," he told Coutre. "Does he know?"

Coutre stared at the whisky.

"That he is dying?" He lifted the glass. "Yes . . . he knows. He knows."

2

Even as the fishermen of the Two Rivers town prepared for the coming lake-trout season, the Wisconsin legislature in the capitol at Madison was also making preparations for the same season. It was the contention of the State Conservation Commission that the lake-trout population decline in the Great Lakes was directly traceable to overfishing by the commercial fishermen; some sort of legislative curb was badly needed.

It cannot be overlooked that in the Great Lakes to the east, namely: Ontario, Huron, and Erie, the lake trout have fallen off in alarming proportions and obviously the same thing will happen in Lakes Michigan and Superior unless measures are taken to protect the trout from the inroads of commercial fishermen.

As the state legislature has jurisdiction over Wisconsin boundary water the Conservation Commission considers it a duty to the people of Wisconsin to recommend that the legislature pass into law a bill requiring that the size of mesh in gill nets be enlarged, thus enabling smaller fish to swim freely through the nets, and thus to grow into large mature fish.

The Conservation Commission notes that commercial fishermen are not always concerned with good conservation practice, being of course more concerned with realizing substantial profits from their business. Nonetheless, the fact remains that the lake trout in Great Lakes waters adjacent to the state of Wisconsin are resources of the state, that is to say, these lake trout belong to the people of Wisconsin and not to any select group, certainly not the commercial fishermen.

Commercial fishing for lake trout off Wisconsin shores is a multimillion-dollar industry and it benefits a great many people in the state. It is not right that a shortsighted selfish group of men realize profits for a time when the long-range view indicates a repetition of the disasters that have befallen the eastern Great Lakes.

This was the meat of the Conservation Commission report to the legislature. Shortly after its presentation a senator from the southern part of the state got on the bandwagon with a bill and began to plump for passage into law.

Politically it was a good safe bill for the southern bloc

as the major share of lake-trout fishing in the state was carried on in the northern areas.

The *Two Rivers Reporter* carried the story about the Conservation Commission and the legislature on the front page. When the Old Man read it he climbed out of bed and got into his pants and went storming downstairs like a sou'wester. His sons were still at the supper table having coffee and cigarettes. Mama was the first to see the Old Man.

"What are you doing with your pants on?" she said.

His sons turned and saw him then and leaped up from the table and crowded around him and everybody began talking at once. It seemed to the Old Man that they were about to carry him bodily back to the bedroom.

Then the Old Man screamed and waved the newspaper like a club.

"Stop treating me like I was crazy!"

"Well," Mama said, "stop acting like one."

The Old Man handed the newspaper to Mama and folded his arms.

"Read," he said, "what it says about the Conservation Commission and the legislature in Madison."

"I don't have my glasses," Mama said.

The Old Man stood sternly like a prophet.

"Somebody," he said, "read it to her."

The brothers clustered around the paper; Roger found the story and hesitatingly read it out loud. His dark proud face was frowning.

When he finished, they all looked at the Old Man.

"What does it mean?" Mama asked.

"It means we are in trouble," the Old Man said. "Everyone of us commercial fishermen who has gill nets out for the trout!" LeMere watched Roger closely. *He wants to be boss. Perhaps this is his chance.*

"Can they do this, Pa?" Roger asked.

The Old Man looked around at his sons. He answered Roger's question without speaking, walking past them, sitting down at the table; he asked Mama if she had coffee.

She brought his cup and began to pour and the Old Man's sons slowly seated themselves again, watching him. He sipped the hot coffee. He set it down and settled forward.

"Yes, they can do it all right," he said quietly to Roger. "Give me a cigarette somebody."

Roger gave the Old Man a cigarette and lit it for him with the worn Zippo. LeMere inhaled and Mama glared.

"You know what Doctor Coutre told you," she said.

"Yes, I know all right," the Old Man said. "Only I was not fighting the whole state of Wisconsin then."

Mama turned and went back to the kitchen.

The Old Man looked around the table and surveyed his sons. *They don't know what to do, he thought.* Roger sat like a prize fighter on a stool, loosening his shoulders, waiting for something to swing at. Old LeMere almost smiled. Indian wrestling in the river-front beer joints was an accomplishment of sorts—but nobody was going to impress the learned lawmakers in Madison by pounding the table and rolling up a sleeve.

The twins, Gabriel and Raphael, sat in silence, trying to look interested. What the hell, the Old Man felt. At twenty years of age, with every tooth still in your head and curly sideburns like a movie star, it was pretty hard to get worked up about little things like laws and fish nets. Le-

Mere could read those baby blue eyes like a newspaper. Sure as hell they were thinking of women. They were always thinking of women, the young bastards.

"Gabriel," the Old Man asked, "is there a dance tonight?"

"Yes, Pa." The even white teeth flashed in surprise. "At Mishicot."

Raphael grinned broadly. At Mishicot. That means polkas and plenty of beer. Jesus, lock up your women; and, Katy, bar the door.

At the far end of the table, the boy Reuben caught the Old Man's eyes. Ah, little Bébé. At ten years of age, he had the body of a bird and the heart of a girl. The Old Man gave his baby a secret wink.

"Well, the way I see this business," the Old Man said, "somebody has to go to Madison. Somebody to represent the fishermen and go to Madison and talk against this bill."

"What good will that do?" Roger asked. "You can't talk to those politics bastards."

The twins shook their heads and mumbled in agreement.

"Well, now," the Old Man said, looking at Roger, "what would you do about this thing?"

"I don't know." He stretched his long frame uncomfortably, searching for words. "I don't know for sure, Pa. But sure as hell we have to do a lot more than just talk."

"That's right, Pa," Raphael said. "Talking is no good at all."

"Hell, no," Gabriel said.

The Old Man sat smoking.

"I want to have a meeting," he said. "We must have all the fishermen along this beach at the meeting and we will talk."

"That's nothing," Roger said.

"I want to have a meeting," the Old Man said. "We shall see."

Roger glared at his brothers and at the Old Man; no one said anything.

"Christ, Pa. They're all busy with the spring setup," Roger said. "Nobody will have any time anyway."

"I want you to call them and tell them I want a meeting. Or must I call them myself?"

No one said anything and the only sound in the room was the sound of the Lake Michigan surf boiling onto the beach beyond the dunes.

"I'll call them," Roger said. "But I know damn well what they're going to say." He smashed out his cigarette, slammed back his chair and stood up.

"What," he asked, "do you want me to say?"

"Tell them I want a meeting about this net Bill. Tell them to meet here at the house."

"All right. When?"

"Right away. Tonight."

"Tonight!" Roger stared at the Old Man. "That's crazy, Pa. I can't tell them that."

The Old Man started to get up.

"I will tell them myself," he said. The twins watched him and didn't say anything. Mama came in from the kitchen.

Roger moved toward the hall where the telephone was. "Okay, okay, I'll call them."

The Old Man settled back in his chair; he put out his cigarette and asked Reuben to go fetch his pipe and tobacco.

The boy scurried into the front room to the fireplace mantel. He reached up for the Canadian briar and the whole can of Prince Albert. When he returned Roger was talking on the telephone. The Old Man was sitting with his hands folded. Mama was speaking.

"You know what the doctor said," she was saying angrily. She turned to her sons. "You all know what the doctor—" She stopped in the middle of her sentence as Reuben walked into the room and took the pipe and tobacco to the Old Man.

The Old Man thanked him and patted his head and Reuben went back to his chair. His brothers stared down at their coffee cups as the Old Man packed up his pipe. Mama was just standing over him. Reuben tried to think if he had heard the doctor say anything special.

"Papa," he asked loudly, "what about the doctor?"

Mama looked at him quickly. His brothers looked at him. Finally, very slowly the Old Man looked at him, clamping on the pipestem, sucking down the bowl pack, getting ready to light it.

"Did the doctor say something special?" Reuben asked. His voice shrilled.

The Old Man got the pipe going strong. There were blue clouds of smoke around his head. He leaned forward and looked at Reuben.

"Now then, Bébé," he said, "what about the doctor?"

The boy said he did not know anything about the doctor at all.

"That is a true statement of fact," the Old Man said. "You do not know about the doctor because no one here thinks you are a man. If they thought you were a man then you would know about the doctor." He pulled the pipe from his mouth and stared at the bowl. "Are you a man, Bébé?"

The boy did not know what the Old Man was talking about but it made Mama mad.

"What foolishment are you filling the boy with?" she snapped. "What good will it do for him to know?"

"Even a minnow learns from the big fish, Mama. This will do him every good in the world."

Mama turned her head sharply to one side and the boy knew that for a sure sign that she was very angry.

"Bébé," the Old Man said, "I believe you are a man. Or perhaps I say this only to be the first to say it. A man must see things always as they are. He must not pretend things are not that way."

He paused and looked at the boy and though he had listened carefully to every word, the boy still did not know what his father was talking about.

"Everything in this world, Bébé. Everything that is living must one day die. That is the way things are."

Reuben got a cold feeling inside his chest and he remembered when his school class all had to go to the funeral mass for the little girl who had fallen into the river last year and drowned below the bridge. Mama left the room then and the Old Man did not talk but watched her go.

"No one knows when he is going to die, Bébé. I cannot tell you and you cannot tell me. Some people do not like to think about dying at all. But that is pretending. Anyway, no one can tell for sure when you will die. Except perhaps a person like a doctor, Bébé."

"Did the doctor say you were going to die, Papa?"

"Yes, Bébé. That is what the doctor said."

"When?" he asked.

The Old Man looked at him and smiled.

"That is what I asked him too," he said. "My very first question. Tell me now, Bébé. Do you feel a little bigger now? Do you feel like a man at all?"

The boy was so confused he did not know what to say. Gabriel sat quietly, his hands folded, his eyes on his father. Raphael was biting the nail of his forefinger, shifting restlessly. The Old Man seemed to be the only happy person there. Then the Old Man beckoned to Reuben with his pipe. He went to stand at his father's side.

"It is the heart," he said fixing Reuben's fingers on his thick, corded wrist. "Feel it now for a moment."

No one moved and the beat of his father's heart pounded up the boy's arm like a man hammering on a bent nail and stopping and hammering again.

"The doctor says that very soon, this . . . this hammering will stop. Then I will be dead. It is very much like the old engine in the fish tug before we got the new one. It simply runs down and breaks, Bébé. That is all. That is living, or rather, that is dying."

Before Reuben could say anything Roger walked in from the hall, slumped into his chair and lighted a cigarette.

"Damn right," he said. "I told you they wouldn't come."

The Old Man took his wrist away from the boy.

"What do you mean, they won't come?"

"That's the whole story, Pa. They're not going to come for a meeting, that's all."

"What did you ask them? What did you tell them? Did you tell them that I want to have a meeting here?"

"Christ, Pa. I told them exactly what you told me to tell them. And they're not going to come for a meeting."

The Old Man seemed to sag in his chair, like a channel buoy half buried in rough weather.

"They are not coming," he said.

No one said anything and the Old Man just stared.

"Why won't they come?" the Old Man asked. His voice was very soft.

"They say it won't do any good," Roger said. "They're busy with the spring setup. They don't have time to go to Madison. They don't think you can fight the state anyway."

"They all say this?" the Old Man asked. "Smitty. Gunnar. Jacques. Dussault. All of them? They all say this?"

"All of them," Roger said.

The Old Man hunched forward slowly. He put his pipe down and took another cigarette and stared, tapping the cigarette on the table top.

Reuben looked around at his brothers and then Mama came in with some more coffee. She stopped next to the Old Man and asked him what he was going to do.

"I am going to pray a little bit, Mama," he said. "I am going to pray and think a little bit and not talk too much. Then I am going to raise a holy hell with those dumb bastards!"

"What do you mean?" Mama asked.

"I mean only," the Old Man said, "if all of them will not come here, then all right, I will go to them."

"In your condition!" Mama said. "Are you gone crazy in your old age?"

"Pa," Roger said, "they're right. It's a waste of time. You can't fight the state."

"Speak for *them,* not for *me!*" the Old Man said. "I can fight the state all right. With them or without them."

The Old Man got to his feet quickly and took the back of the chair. He was starting for the telephone when it happened. He heard Mama's angry voice in his ears but he could not see her because suddenly there was a pinky blackness in front of his eyes and a sharpness in the middle of his chest like a gaff hook. He groped for the chair and Mama's voice sounded like a gull screaming on the wind and the gaff hook came again and again and then the gull screams and the wind and the hook rose like a long heavy breaker and then there was nothing at all.

Doctor Coutre came immediately and with him Father Doucette. The doctor took one look at the Old Man and said the priest better give him the Last Rites. Then he talked to Mama for a long time and that night a cablegram went crossing the Atlantic to Major Germaine LeMere in France.

They stayed in the kitchen drinking coffee and waiting for his answer.

3

Germaine was tired. His six-foot frame throbbed. His legs were asleep and stinging. He had not slept at all since leaving Orly Field and yet he was too keyed up to rest now. He was accustomed to long flights as a pilot but flying as a passenger always sapped and drained him like a long bus ride, and because he had no responsibilities on this flight his thoughts went buffeting him about like strong headwinds. He was tired, dragged out, and his insides felt like a windmilling engine.

He looked at the little blond girl sleeping next to him, her knees drawn up to her chin. The excitement had worn off now, the excitement that had begun in Paris with the jangling phone bell and exploded into the whining engines of the Constellation on the Orly apron.

We are going home, Julia. We are going home. To America.

The green eyes squinted against the window glare. After all the years of the planes and the flight plans and the manifests and the check points and the briefings and the hours and the miles and the wind directions and the patterns and the approaches and the landings and the cargoes . . . after all of it . . . after a war and after a few years of peace, he was going home and he was tired and too keyed up to rest. He smoked his cigarette and stroked the little girl's silky long braids.

You could tell a five-year-old that you were going home but you couldn't tell her that someone was dying at home and you waited for her excitement to wear off and after that she would sleep. After Orly and the Azores. The Atlantic and Gander. After Idlewild. She would sleep and then there would be only Midway in Chicago, the last landing. The last lap of the inevitable journey and there would be old Doctor Coutre waiting. Thirty-four years ago Coutre brought you into the world and now the cycle was complete. A man lives his life and it is a Great Circle Route and he returns . . . After a long, long flight he returns. He brushed the ashes from his uniform and stared out at the sky.

They were over the Middle West now and the darkness was coming on in the valleys far below and lights winked on despite the fact that the Constellation still flew in sunlight. He remembered when he was in high school before the war the Holy Name retreat he had gone to in the Marquette football stadium in Milwaukee. The priest had used a loud-speaker system to reach the crowd in the stands, when it was dark he had asked each man to strike a match on signal. The flare was startling. A huge shocked gasp came from the crowd as if from one man. It was as though a giant star shell had exploded in the stadium and hung there, lingering.

"A prayer is like a match flame," the priest had said. "A great many prayers are a blaze. There is strength in men working together, praying together. There is power to bring light into the dark places."

He wondered now how many men there in the stadium that night had remembered the priest and his matches when they had gone into the dark places of this world. He felt that many of them would have remembered during the war. That was the kind of thing war made a man remember.

The little girl stirred and found her thumb. Germaine realized that the priest and the stadium and the matches were a long time ago. That all belonged to a time before this little girl . . . before this time.

He wondered about the Old Man now and what his chances were. And what if it was all too late. The thought startled him. My God, there were so many things he had to tell the Old Man. *So* many years to make up for. He wanted very much to see the Old Man face to face and clasp the tough hands once more. And in the throats of the powerful engines, the *too late too late too late* repeated endlessly. Repeated and then became an incoherent moaning.

He finished his cigarette as the smiling stewardess came by, whispering. The FASTEN SEAT BELTS sign flashed on above the NO SMOKING. He strapped in the sleeping child and then himself. He held the small body firmly as the city of Chicago lighted the sky like a fire and then the plane swung wide into the approach pattern and slowly, gently flew down into the blaze.

Germaine came through the gate carrying the sleeping child in his arms. Doctor Coutre was waiting and there was a priest with him and Germaine knew it had to be Father Joe. He felt the tension, took a deep breath and then he felt a kind of relief washing through him like warm water. So, he told himself, it might as well begin here and now. This is all part of coming home. He gave them a warm grin.

They each threw an arm around him and stared into his tanned face silently.

"Gray hair," Father Joe murmured. "Gray hair, he has now."

"At the temples only," Doctor Coutre said. "That is distinguished-looking."

Then they looked at him closely and at the fair little girl. Germaine read the questions in their eyes.

"Her name is Julia," he said softly. "She's my daughter."

The traffic of the world's busiest airport was swirling and eddying around them and they stood like isolated islands.

Finally the doctor said, "Baggage. We better go pick up your baggage."

They moved through the lobby and into the bustling corridor where faces flowed past them.

4

They had left Chicago far behind and then Milwaukee and were heading up Highway 141 for Two Rivers. Germaine was driving now, relieved to be doing something with his hands. He held the station wagon at an even sixty as the road unwound like a spool of ribbon in the headlight beams. Beside him, Doctor Coutre was slumped, smoking. They had changed positions in Milwaukee and in the rear seat Father Joe sat next to the sleeping Julia.

The sharp spring air came in cold and cleansing and they could hear the breakers of Lake Michigan pounding into the open beach on their right.

"No moon," the doctor said, "and rough. A good night for lifting fish nets, huh, Germaine?"

"A good night," came Father Joe's deepest voice, "for

poachers and pirates and illegal fishermen. Doctor Coutre, you have the soul of a crook."

Germaine smiled a little, found a cigarette and punched the dash lighter. It had been a long time since he had been in a boat on a night like this in the fish grounds. He had been with the Old Man and Roger and they had lifted the pot net by hand and with it a great illegal sturgeon. It had all been a long time ago. The lighter popped.

"A good night all right," he said. He half-turned. "Remember, Father, the Old Man always called a night like this God's gift to fishermen."

"I remember," the priest said.

"He still does," the doctor said.

"Ah," the priest said. "Your Father."

Germaine had come home from half a world away for this moment. In the liquid flowing silence he braced himself like a swimmner in strong current and fought for headway.

"The Old Man," he said. "How is he?"

Outside the wind ran like a river.

"He is a sick man," Doctor Coutre said. "I do not like to think about the rest of it."

"His heart?" Germaine said.

He could see the doctor nodding silently, his cigarette glowing.

"Yes," the doctor said. "His heart. Other things."

Father Doucette was leaning forward.

"Aggravation," he said. "He has too much aggravation with the fishing."

"This is true," the doctor said. "He is a tired man. His heart is tired. The fishing has taken everything out of him."

"Everything?"

"His strength. His heart." The doctor stopped and his voice was a deep sigh. "He drove himself too much."

Germaine clutched the wheel tightly.

"What are his chances?"

"He has heart damage. And he is tired."

"Will he live?"

"It is too early to tell. We need more tests. Examinations. I took him to the hospital."

He thought about the Old Man, his father, beached. Driven high onto his shore by the great waters. Driven like a derelict hull to grow mushy and cork-soft with the dry rot.

"His fishing is over," the doctor said. "He should have stopped long ago."

"He told me many times," the priest said. "He could not stop. There was no one else."

Germaine half turned sharply.

"What do you mean, no one else?"

"To take over," the priest said. "There was no one."

"Roger," Germaine said. "There was Roger. Raphael. Gabriel. They're men now."

"Your father told me many times. There was no one, Germaine."

Doctor Coutre leaned forward and crushed out his cigarette.

"Oh, he has a chance. A good chance. But no more fishing for him. No matter what. He must rest, take it easy."

Germaine remembered the Old Man and all the four o'clock mornings. Slickered and booted and tall in the pilothouse and swinging the fish tug out into the rolling waters of the open lake. He saw the Old Man, driving spiles and tarring nets and the great hands gutting lake trout. His huge rope-burned hands moving like hawk wings when the tug wallowed over the fish grounds and the work was fast and heavy and there was no time to think. *He must rest, the doctor said, take it easy.*

"It will kill him to be on the beach," Germaine said.

"Perhaps," Doctor Coutre said. "It will most certainly kill him to fish. It's over for him, Germaine. Finished."

"You know," Father Doucette said, "I used to keep after him to give up the fishing and go someplace. He always said he would rather die all at once in his fish boots than piecemeal in some strange hotel. But I think he would have retired long ago if there was *someone* here."

"Someone?" Germaine asked.

"Well," the priest said. "You. Someone like you. I know he always wanted that. He wanted his sons to love the fishing, the way he did. You loved it that way, Germaine."

He glanced in the mirror and caught a quick flash of the priest's face.

"So," Father Doucette said. "It is never too late."

Germaine dragged on the cigarette. Now he knew what the priest was getting at.

"My life is not on the fishermen's beach," he said. "I didn't come back to take over the Old Man's business."

"Germaine," the priest said, "you may *have* to."

Germaine couldn't keep the anger out of his voice.

"Dammit, Father. Roger, Gabriel, Raphael. They are fishermen. Let them do it. My life is not here."

There was a long silence. "All right," the priest said. "Your life is not here. All right."

Doctor Coutre leaned forward and touched Germaine on the knee gently.

"You must forgive the old men," he said. "We are always sticking our noses into the business of young men."

"That's all right, Doctor."

"Don't be angry."

"No, of course not."

"And please forgive us."

"There's nothing to forgive, Doctor."

"Good," the doctor said. Then he slumped down into his traveling position and adjusted himself. "Good," he said again. "Now we would like to know all about the little girl. We old men."

Germaine didn't say anything.

"I think we have shown remarkable patience," the doctor said. "Wouldn't you say so, Joe?"

"Yes," the priest said. "I would certainly say so."

"I want to tell you," Germaine said. "Only I don't know where to begin."

"Well," the priest said, "we are just a couple of small-town bachelors, wouldn't you say so, Doctor?"

"We are provincial rubes," the doctor said.

"And she is such a beautiful child," the priest went on.

"You could start with her mother, Germaine," the doctor said softly.

The doctor was right. It had started with her.

They were talking about Erika now and in his mind's eye, Germaine saw her very clearly for a minute as he had seen her in a thousand fleeting glimpses on a thousand flights. Her eyes filled the sky. Her laughter ran on the wind. She had given him love and laughter and her life continued now in the body of their child. It had always hurt him to remember Erika. Now he wanted these friends from the old days to know about her.

"Her name was Erika," he began. "She was a German

National. We met in North Africa during the war."

He could sense the priest and the doctor settling themselves; his mind flew its direct lifting course back through the years like a climbing earth-free wing.

"She never even saw Julie," he said. "She died in childbirth."

The men shook their heads and grunted softly. Germaine was grateful for the silence.

"We were never married," he said finally. "I might as well start the story here. Right here."

The child Julia stirred and Father Doucette reached over and stroked her head slowly and Doctor Coutre smoked and watched the unraveling road. Germaine widened his eyes briefly. Then his voice was low and far away as he spoke to them of Erika.

When he had finished talking they were near Manitowoc, and he realized suddenly that he had been talking for a very long time. He had kept it all inside and sooner or later it was bound to burst forth like a dam crumbling and he would wind up talking the ears off someone all night long.

He had felt alone all the while he was talking and now that it was over he did not feel alone any more and the presence of the doctor and the priest bothered him a little bit now.

"I'm sorry," he said. "I got all wound up."

"You were gone a long time," the doctor said. "That's a long story." They smoked then and sat quietly and Germaine knew what the priest was going to say before he said it.

"The little girl," Father Joe began slowly. "She is not baptized?"

"No, Father. She is not baptized."

"Why not, in God's name?"

"I thought I made that pretty clear, Father."

"You lost your faith?"

"That's right."

"And because you lost yours you propose to withhold hers."

"I don't see that that follows. You make it sound like I'm punishing her."

"Aren't you?"

It was no good talking about it, he knew. He had been over it a thousand times with himself and he knew how he saw the situation. He knew that a Catholic priest wasn't going to see it in the same way at all and it was no good talking.

"No," he said. "I'm not punishing her."

"Germaine," the priest said, "I always felt that it would be something like this. I knew you too well to think that you would not have your own good reasons for staying away. Times of strife and upheaval . . . war, armies. A woman. They shake the faith of many men. And many men lose their faith. But Germaine, we are talking in terms of souls now. Immortal souls."

"Father, I can't bring her up Catholic."

"You mean you won't."

"All right then. I won't."

"Germaine, she has an immortal soul."

"A *Catholic* soul?"

"Yes, a *Catholic* soul."

"I say no." He drew on his cigarette and it calmed him. He didn't want to talk about it. He knew it wouldn't get them anywhere and he knew the priest wanted to talk about it now. He waited.

"It's your duty to have her baptized, Germaine."

"Father, it's my duty to feed her and raise her and love her, yes. And I'll tell you how I know about that duty. Because my heart says yes, that's my duty. She's my flesh and blood. I'm all she has. But my heart doesn't say anything about baptizing her. It doesn't say anything about Catholicism. Father, I don't believe. I just don't believe."

Doctor Coutre coughed then. He cleared his throat and spoke very loudly.

"I think it's a little late for all this weighty discussion tonight, gentlemen." He cleared his throat again with a hacking cough. "You know," he said, "I should see a good doctor."

The tension was relieved and Germaine was grateful to him. He could feel the priest's righteous anger in the darkness.

"You must understand, Father," he said. "I don't want to hurt you."

"I understand that," the priest said. "It's not me you're hurting, Germaine."

Germaine saw the doctor's head tilt and he half turned expecting to see his eyes, but the doctor was staring at the road and the stark narrow sign marked TWO RIVERS. In the east, the false dawn was billowing out like a purse seine and starting to drag the lake. Germaine's thoughts too dragged like nets and caught and took hold of the old familiar things. This shore line. This road. That sign. From the sign he knew that it was seven miles to the white frame house at the fringe of the Point Beach Forest. Seven miles and a lifetime. The net was tightening on him now, holding him and pulling him against the current. Seven miles. As the crow flies and the sea gull flies and the flier flies. He was getting a little giddy inside; he could feel the butterflies and it was all coming back, bobbing like cork floats and he wanted to tell them how he felt but he kept it all inside. He even thought of Ginny Dussault again. How many times had they driven along this very road, dreaming dreams for their future.

"Is somebody meeting us in town?" he asked. "Roger or somebody to drive us out?"

"No," the doctor said, sitting up. "No. Just keep driving the old wagon."

"Why didn't somebody meet us?"

"Well," the doctor said, "they don't know you're coming."

"What?"

"Oh, your mother knows. Of course. She wanted it this way, Germaine. She has her reasons."

Germaine drove through the empty silent town.

"The Old Man doesn't know I'm coming," he said. "No one knows. Is that it?"

"Yes," the doctor said. "That's it."

She had her reasons, the doctor had said. It could be his mother was ashamed of him or afraid of him or a lot of things. Yes. It could be a lot of things. He had been away so long it certainly could be a lot of things. Germaine got a bad feeling just then and the nets tightened and he felt like a fish. Trapped and helpless.

"She's expecting us," he said, "my mother?"

"Your mother," the doctor said looking at his watch, "is

expecting you. I'd bet my life she's had the coffee on for hours."

He thought about his mother sitting coolly efficient, her black hair pulled into a tight bun, waiting in the warm kitchen, watching the clock, listening for a station wagon. He thought of the Old Man in the hospital, the doctor and the priest, and of Erika, and of little Julie sleeping in the rear seat. He drove through the rest of the town without a word; then he stopped at the deserted intersection and turned onto the lake road that ran hard and rattling as an anchor chain back into the Old Man's beach.

5

They waited in the wagon so he could be alone with his mother a little.

He walked hesitantly at first, feeling the cold fresh wind on his face, the heavy pine forest smell in his nose. And then he was a little boy again racing across the beach and taking all the back steps in one floating glide and bursting, flushed, into the sweet kitchen where she waited.

She had aged. He had not seen her for six years and he realized with immediate shock that all this time her unchanging picture in his mind's eye had been an untrue picture belonging to an earlier time, an earlier face, and he knew the terrible truth that the years had not been kind to his mother. The fisherman's beach had worn her away as the pounding waters wore away the glacier rocks.

A deep sadness swept over him; he went to her, held her. She cried in his arms.

"I knew you would come," she repeated over and over. "I knew. I knew."

It swept over him again, that deep self-accusing sadness. It came as a great wave and buried him and drowned him and he knew that she had aged so because of him, and he knew that there were no words to put it right. His words would never brush away the hard harsh work of time. Her hair, once proud and black, now lay limp as a dead gull's wing. Her face webbed and strung in unyielding lines. And her eyes. He had seen eyes with the same expression during the war. Gethsemane. They had seen sorrow and they had seen too much and now they wanted surcease.

He held her tightly. He closed his eyes and he cried.

Then she was looking up at him, patting his cheek and pushing him away and smiling a little bit.

"He will be so happy to see you," she said. "So happy, Germaine."

He didn't say anything.

"I know it," she said. "It will be all right."

"Mama," he said. "I'm sorry, Mama. For everything."

She caressed his face with both hands.

"I know," she said. "It will be all right. Now enough."

She got a frying pan out of the stove drawer. "You better call in Father Joe and the doctor. They are probably starved. And you too. Would you like ham and eggs?"

"Mama, I want to talk to you first."

"They're starved, Germaine. We can talk while you eat."

"Yes," he said. "All right."

He went to the door and waved to the men in the

station wagon. The doctor waved back and slowly got out. Germaine stood at the door watching.

"Mama," he said. He wanted to find the words to tell her about Julia but the words wouldn't come. Thousands of miles away, he had been able to deny the knowledge that he had given this woman many bad moments. Now, face to face, he knew that they had piled like the stones of a cairn into bad years and she did not deserve another bad moment in this life. Yet that moment was ticking up the pathway now with every stroke of the big kitchen clock and he was powerless.

It was like waiting for a parachute to open or a bomb to detonate. He watched the three strangers—two old men and a little blond girl—getting out of the station wagon. The giddy feeling hit him again as in an aircraft. In the air he had always known the exact moment the plane passed the point of no return; a pilot had to be very careful about that. Somehow, he had crossed that point in his own personal life long ago and he had not been careful in marking it and now he could not go back. At this very moment he wanted desperately to go back to his youth because it was a good time and not a lonely time and a young man knew damned well that he was going to live forever. Youth was the time of first things in life. The first time in the marsh flats after mallards. The first time in the snowy woods with a rifle. The first time with a girl. He looked at his daughter being carried in the old priest's arms.

Then they were coming into the kitchen and his daughter was running to him. He bent down to meet her and he watched his mother turn from the stove and stare at the child.

"Daddy, Daddy," Julia said, "where were you?"

He held her. "It's all right, honey. It's all right."

The doctor had closed the door and was standing next to the priest. They were watching his mother.

He took the little girl by the hand and turned her. "This lady is my mother," he said. "She's your grandma."

Julia's blue eyes watched the old woman. His mother put down the spatula and wiped her hands on her apron. Then she moved quickly to the child.

"This is Julia," he said. "She's mine, Mama." Germaine got to his feet. His mother looked at Julia without moving; then she flung her arms around the little girl and began to cry as she held her tightly.

Germaine glanced at the doctor and the priest and they were watching him closely. The doctor was nodding his head and winking his eye to Germaine, and then he nudged the priest and the two men moved over to the breakfast table and seated themselves. Germaine knelt and held his mother and his daughter both together in his arms.

They had finished breakfast and Mama was refilling their coffee cups when Doctor Coutre came back from the telephone in the hall.

"He had a good night," he said. "You can see him today, Germaine."

"Good," Germaine said. "Good."

"No more coffee for me, Martha," the doctor said. "We should be going now, Joe."

"Yes," the priest said. "All right."

Father Joe got to his feet and ground out his cigarette and joined the doctor.

"I only wish I could have eaten," the priest said. "But I have Mass."

"I know, Father. Thank you for everything."

The priest touched her arm.

"You'll have him out of the hospital in no time, Martha."

Germaine sensed that the priest wanted to say more so he pushed back his chair and stood up.

"I'll get our bags out of the wagon," he told them. He went out of the kitchen into the sharp blowing dawn of the beachlands and the heavy nose-filling odor of tarred nets.

This place is where I was born, Erika, and my people work this beach and this is part of our Julia too.

The sky was gray as gun metal and the water was green and pus-colored and boiling out of the north. On the horizon an ore carrier was heading down from the Lakehead to the steel mills around Chicago. He remembered that an eternity ago Erika had been with him at another beach and they had spent his leave in the little house near the sea. They used to sit for hours watching the water and the gulls. He had told of this very place of how in the summertime it was sand and spray into everything. Of winter snows piling up like mountains on the beachlands. Of how clean everything was.

"You will take me with you?" she had asked.

Yes, he had told her. He would take her there.

He closed up the back of the station wagon and lifted the B-4 bags. The doctor and the priest were there.

"It's all right," the doctor said. "They're going to love each other."

"That little one talks a blue streak," the priest said. "They're sounding like my Ladies' Sodality."

They were silent.

"Thank you for everything," Germaine said. "You've been very kind. Both of you."

"Well," the priest said, "God works in many ways. He brought you back, Germaine. Both of you. You belong here."

"Come on, Joe," the doctor said. "Give you an inch and you're building a new church."

Germaine set down the bags and shook their hands and thanked them again. Then he watched the car turn around on the hard, rattling road and they were gone. He picked up the bags and walked slowly toward his father's house.

6

The wall clock in the kitchen was showing eight o'clock when his mother came back from her bedroom. She brought the coffeepot from the stove and refilled his cup and then her own.

"She's sleeping like an angel now. I put her in my bed."

Germaine unfastened his blouse.

"You're sure it's all right, Mama," he said. "I don't want us to be any trouble."

"Of course it's all right," she said. "This is your house too, Germaine. It always was."

His mother was watching him closely now.

"You're tired," she said. "You can take one of the twin beds in Reuben's room. You should sleep a little while, Germaine."

He took a cigarette from the pack on the table.

"I could use some sleep, Mama. But I want to see Pa."

"First, sleep," she said. "We can go to the hospital this afternoon."

"Don't let me sleep through, Mama. Really."

"All right."

"Promise?"

"Yes, I promise."

"Good."

He caught himself yawning a little and tried to stifle it.

"I guess it's all catching up on me, Mama. I'm sorry."

She looked at him.

"You have had a long journey, my son. A long journey."

He smiled at her and he tried to make it a tender smile; he didn't know what to say.

"Is that why you stayed away from us, Germaine? Because of the little girl?"

The crow's-feet deepened around his green eyes.

"I guess she's part of it, Mama. I don't know."

"Your father felt it was something like this but he could not understand why you stayed away. Night after night he would lie next to me and he could not sleep. Night after night he would ask God why you had turned against your family."

Germaine lowered his head, his hands touching the gray temples.

"Mama, I didn't turn against my family."

"You had your reasons, your father would say. Your life was your concern. But he gave you life, Germaine. He could not forget that you were his son."

"Mama—"

He tried to interrupt, to apologize and ask forgiveness

but she kept on speaking and would not be stopped.

"Night after night, Germaine, he would ask me how he had failed you. Where had he gone wrong with you. What he had done that was so terrible that his oldest son should ignore him like a dead man. The first years he fought with himself like a man possessed and then there were no answers for him. Then one night he could not keep it inside any longer. He cried on my shoulder like a baby. My God, Germaine. Your father. The strongest, bravest man I have ever known. He cried over you like a baby. Honest to God, I think you broke your father's heart, Germaine. And he only wanted you to love him." She was crying softly now. "That's all we ever wanted from you, Germaine. Your love."

"I'm sorry, Mama. I'm sorry. Please. Please don't cry any more."

"I wish you could have seen your father cry."

He held his mother and didn't say anything. He knew that she was crying for his father and for herself and for the little boy who was their oldest son.

He remembered the Communion Sundays he had made for her and the First Fridays and the Novenas and the rosaries recited and the nightly prayers to God to keep her.

Holy Mary, Mother of God, pray for us sinners. Now and at the hour of our death. Amen.

A long time ago the prayers had come easily to his lips. His generation had been altar boys then. In their black, baggy cassocks they looked like little priests and they were all very close to God.

The mothers of the Sodality would come to see them

serve the Mass. The women would be thinking that one day the boys would be real priests and come back to the parish and say the First Mass here and pass out the little remembrance holy cards with the picture of Jesus on the front holding the white lamb and the shepherd's staff.

He remembered that for funerals the priest and the altar boys walked up the aisle and met the casket and led it back to the front of the church at the sanctuary railing.

One of the altar boys had holy water in a golden pail. One had incense. One had a tall metal crucifix painted black and he stood in behind the casket between the front pews full of the dead person's family all the while the priest talked of Heaven and Hell and Purgatory. Germaine never liked to stand there because from there you would hear the crying very clearly.

Some of the altar boys had remembered all this as soldiers when they bagged up the dead men in the mattress covers and looked to see if they had smoked up all their cigarettes.

Words. Words. Words now empty as deserted rooms and silent cocoons. Their nests were dead, their wings had fled. He had addressed a great many words to God, and now he didn't know if the words had meaning for his mother or for God or for anyone. He knew only that once they had had meaning for a boy.

His mother looked at him now, her face a drying, hardening mask.

"I should not have told you about your father that way. He would not want you to know."

He stroked her face.

"I understand, Mama," he said.

"He takes it as a sign of weakness, your father," she said. "To cry. I have never told anyone. Not anyone."

She reached up and touched his temples.

"You are still our son, Germaine. This is still your home."

He bent his head and she held him.

"The past is past," she said. "He will be so glad to see you, Germaine. So glad."

Then she kissed him on the forehead and lifted his face.

"I knew you would come back. I prayed, Germaine."

He kissed her on the cheek and she stroked his hair.

"Now you must sleep," she said. "You can see your brothers later."

He got to his feet and lifted her face.

"Thank you, Mama, for . . . both of us . . ."

She smiled. "You are both welcome here, Germaine. Both of you."

He finished his coffee and put out his cigarette and he took a deep long breath. Then he picked up the remaining B-4 bag and started for the stairway.

"Reuben's room?" he said again. "It's still the same one?"

"Yes," she said. "The same one. It is all ready. I put clean bedding and I will tell the boys not to wake you. And don't worry about the child."

He watched her and he didn't know what to say to her.

"You better go," she said. "They'll be coming down to breakfast soon like a herd of wild horses."

They looked at each other for a long time and when she spoke her voice was soft and low and sweet as a warm wind.

"Father Joe and the doctor told me . . . I'm sorry about the child's mother. I'm sorry she died."

He watched her face and suddenly it seemed a younger face, a gentler face. It was as if he was seeing Erika's face. He stared at his mother and then slowly turned away and started up the stairs.

The boy Reuben was aware of movement downstairs. He could hear dishes clattering and could smell strong coffee. His mother was fixing breakfast for his brothers and he knew that it was morning. Then he remembered that his father was in the hospital. He leaped out of bed and knelt down and said his morning prayers. He squeezed his eyes tightly and said two Our Fathers and three Hail Marys and Glory Be's and he said them all for his father.

"And please, God, don't let Papa die," he said. "Please."

He made the Sign of the Cross and opened his eyes.

Then he heard the slow, even, breathing sound from across the room in the other bed. He whirled, frightened. He padded across the room and bent over the sleeping figure. The man was sleeping face down in the pillow and he couldn't see the face. The boy's wide eyes swept the room; he saw the large clothes neatly hung on the straight-back chair by the window.

Reuben moved to the chair like an animal.

He saw the Army officer's blouse hanging from the chair and the ribbons and the overseas bars and the shining wings on the left breast. He dashed back to the bed and bent himself way over and tried to see the face.

It was Germaine. It had to be Germaine!

He climbed into his bluejeans; he was shaking with excitement as he let himself out the door and went tearing into his brothers' rooms. Gabriel's bed was empty and Raphael's and they were gone. He flew to the next room and Roger's bed was empty too. He ran into the bathroom and it smelled strongly of cigarette smoke. There was no one there.

He flung himself down the steps two at a time and burst into the kitchen like a bomb, his pulse pounding.

His three brothers were all seated at the table eating breakfast and Mama was pouring coffee for them. They all turned and looked at him.

"Bébé," Mama was saying, "you will please get some clothes on you."

"He is a pretty hungry one, that one," Roger laughed. "He was afraid there would be no food."

The twins laughed and kept looking at him.

"He can't be a LeMere," Gabriel said.

"Too scrawny," Raphael said.

"Too skinny," Gabriel said.

"Too late for breakfast," Roger said. They all laughed again. Then Mama spoke.

"Now go dress yourself, Bébé," she said. "And wash first. Scoot, now."

Reuben had caught his breath a little.

"Mama," he said, "Germaine's back, isn't he?"

The brothers were quiet almost instantly and they stared at him and then at Mama.

"He's sleeping in my room, isn't he? Isn't that Germaine, Mama?"

"Yes," she said softly. "That is Germaine. And you are to let him sleep. Now upstairs with you, Bébé, and dress yourself. Quietly now."

Bébé nodded his head and turned and closed the door.

Roger stared after him as Mama took the coffee back to the stove and came back to her chair.

"Germaine," Roger said, his clean-shaven face flushed. "What the hell does *he* want?"

Gabriel and Raphael looked at Mama.

"He wants to see your father," Mama said. "It is his father too."

"Well," Roger said, "he took his good sweet time about it. Where the hell was he all the years Pa needed him?"

"Roger!"

"Well, dammit, it's true," Roger said. "Where was he when Pa needed him?"

"He was in the Army, man," Raphael said.

"There was a war on, Rog," Gabriel said. "Didn't you hear?"

Roger glared. "Sure," he said, "I suppose he figures now that Pa's dying he can step right in and take over the whole shebang."

Gabriel's earnest young face clouded. His voice deepened.

"What've you got? A complex or something?"

Roger leaned forward, one great hand holding the other, his arms bulging.

"You tell me why big brother is back."

Gabriel bit his lip.

"Can't he come back just to see Pa?"

"Pa, my foot," Roger snorted, his jaw thrust out. "I'll tell you why—"

"No," Mama snapped, "I'll tell you why he came back. He came back because I asked him to."

Roger turned and stared at her.

"You asked him to?" he said.

"I called him to come back," she said. "Because his father is dying. That is all. Not to, as you say, take over. I want him to make his peace with your father."

The silence deepened. Gabriel watched her. Raphael bit his forefinger.

"It's not easy for Germaine," she said. "Not easy."

Roger tilted his head and looked at her slyly.

"He never made it easy for you or Pa," he said. "Well, he's not fooling me. I know why he came back."

"You are fooling yourself, Roger," Mama said. "You do not know why he came back."

"I say I do."

"And I say," Mama snapped, "that you do not know what you are talking about."

Roger took a deep breath and looked away from Mama.

"Germaine is my son," she went on, "as much as any of you. And he has as much right here as any of you. You are all brothers and I will not have brother against brother in this house."

Gabriel and Raphael sat quietly, finishing their coffee. Then Roger pushed his chair back from the table.

"We better go to work," he said dully.

The brothers shoved back their chairs and stood up.

"What about Pa?" Raphael asked. He was looking at Mama.

"I'll go to him this afternoon," she said. "With Germaine." She looked at each of them.

"I think your father would want you working a full day on the beach. What do you think?"

"As long as Pa's not in trouble," Gabriel said. "Sure."

"I guess he'd want us to work," Raphael said.

"Well," Roger said. "Let's go. We got a long day."

Mama got to her feet.

"Just one more thing. I am going to show you something now. So you understand that coming home was not easy for Germaine." She looked at Roger and he didn't say anything.

She went to the bedroom door, opened it quietly and looked in. She put her fingers to her lips and motioned them forward.

They looked at each other with puzzled faces, moving quietly across the kitchen. They crowded around the bedroom door.

"What?" Raphael asked.

"It's a kid," Gabriel said.

"A what?"

"A kid. A girl."

"Whose?"

Mama shushed them.

"Germaine's," she said.

They all leaned in at once and filled the doorway and stared.

"Jeeze," Gabriel said. "We're uncles."

Mama slowly closed the door.

"Where'd he get her?" Raphael asked.

"Stupid," Gabriel said. "Where do you think he got her?"

"No," Raphael said. "I mean where did he get her?"

They looked at Mama.

"In North Africa," Mama said.

"Well, I'll be God damned," Raphael said.

"Raphael!"

"I mean I'll be damned, Mama."

"How long's he had her?" Raphael asked. "I mean she looks pretty big."

"She's five years old," Mama said. "Her name is Julia."

Gabriel and Raphael looked at each other and then at Roger who was standing and finishing his coffee.

"This, I take it," he said, "means that Germaine has *married* himself a wife." He looked at Mama but she didn't say anything. Roger raised a dark eyebrow.

The twins looked at Roger and then at Mama.

"Where's Germaine's wife?" Gabriel asked. "Didn't he bring her?"

"She's dead," Mama said. "She died in childbirth."

The brothers stood awkwardly for a moment. Then they got into their jackets. Roger held the door open and they filed out to the beach.

"I'll be damned," Raphael said.

"Well," Gabriel said. "It'll be nice to have him home."

"Hell, yes," Roger said under his breath. "It'll be a god-damn picnic."

Standing alone Roger looked squarely at Mama for a full moment. There was a knowing smile on his face as he nodded his head slowly. He turned and went out the door; he began to whistle "Rock-a-bye, Baby."

7

They were in the hospital waiting for Doctor Coutre to come down from the Old Man's room. Germaine smoked and watched his mother sitting next to his child.

"I think your father will want to see her," Mama said.

"They probably have rules about children, Mama. Regulations."

"Doctor Coutre makes the regulations," Mama said. "He can make an exception."

Germaine leaned forward in his chair, watching down the empty corridor, smelling the sterile healing smells.

He remembered the time in England when he was flying co-pilot on the crippled Fortress and they had crashed and burned. After he came out of the anesthetic they told him that everybody had gotten out safely but the Inquiry

Board had certain questions about the landing. They took his statement in the hospital and he knew what they were after.

"No," he had lied. He didn't think that the pilot had lost his nerve on the approach.

The investigation went on for a month. By the time the crew was re-assigned, the pilot had been transferred to a desk job back in the States and they never discussed him again. Germaine realized then there was no way around trouble in your life. A man going into trouble was like steel going into the fires and if you had the right stuff the flame tempered you and toughened you and made you strong. If you didn't have the right stuff, you cracked and flawed apart and went back to the slag heap. It was open and shut. Either or. Black and white. And it was inevitable. There was no way around this trouble thing. Sooner or later, a man had to go into the flames.

Then Doctor Coutre was standing before them. He looked fresh as an intern. His suit was pressed, his face shaved closely. He looked very professional.

"All right, folks," the doctor was saying. "Just a little while longer yet. Germaine, you can go in now."

Germaine got to his feet and touched the doctor's arm.

"It's all right?"

"I prepared him the best I could," Doctor Coutre half-whispered. "He wants to see you alone."

Germaine looked at the little girl and stroked her fine yellow hair.

"You wait here with Grandma, honey."

Julia's blue eyes clouded.

"I want to come too," she said.

"Not right now."

"I want to."

"In a little while, honey."

Doctor Coutre pointed to the clock.

"Just five or ten minutes, Julia."

"When the big hand is on two?"

"That's right."

"All right," she said. "When the big hand is on two, Daddy."

She put her thumb in her mouth and Germaine and the doctor went down the corridor slowly.

"She sucks her thumb a lot," Germaine said. "I guess she's insecure."

The doctor smiled.

"That's what they say these days. I wouldn't worry about it too much. I smoke a pipe myself." He glanced at Germaine. "Your father. He's still my patient and I'm still his doctor. Sometimes you can't tell about shock on a heart condition. Anyway I wanted him to be prepared. I told him about the little girl. I hope you don't mind."

"No," Germaine said. "No, I don't mind. What did he say?"

"He didn't say anything. Just that he wants to see you alone."

"How did he take it?"

"How does your father take anything? He's not the kind of man to die in bed."

They reached the end of the main corridor and the doctor steered him to the right.

"I don't know how your heart is, Germaine, but I think you're in for a shock too."

"Why? What's the matter?"

"Well, I think your father wants you to take over the fishing."

"Is that what he said?"

"No. He didn't say anything. But I know him like a book. He's got that foxy look in his eyes."

"I can't do that, Doctor."

"Well, that's your business. But I certainly wouldn't tell him that now in so many words."

The doctor stopped walking. He motioned to a half-opened door ahead of them. Then he patted Germaine on the arm.

"I'll wait here," he said.

Germaine nodded. He took a deep breath and stepped into the room.

The Old Man was facing toward the window and the rectangular piece of gray spring sky. He looked long and thin and terribly still. Germaine remembered what his mother had said about the Old Man crying over him in the night. He stood silently staring down at the bed. His father turned slowly and looked at him.

Germaine stared into the old wind-burned face. There was a wetness around the deep green eyes and the Old Man was blinking a little bit and trying hard not to cry. The kind mouth was moving and working but there were no words.

He moved to the bed quickly and took the Old Man's hands in his; he bent his head and they held each other and didn't say anything. Germaine held the Old Man's scarred hands and he felt the years in them. The seasons of the fisherman. Good and bad and inbetween. The dartings of the trapped fish bodies driving hard into the steel strands of the pot nets. The balance of life and death in this great lake; the small hunted by the large and the large hunted by the larger, going on and on until there was no end to the dying in these deep waters. The short lives, savage and constantly exploding like summer storms. A fisherman knew the nature of nets and traps and death; he knew full well that death came swimming in his wake. Death held no surprises for him.

"Germaine," the Old Man whispered. "Germaine."

Then he pulled his hands away and wiped his eyes.

"Fine thing for two grown men," he said. "Acting like a couple of old women."

He ran his hand over his face again, snorting and snuffling.

"We should have a drink on this, Major," he stopped and raised his voice, "but that damned Coutre runs a nursery school. You hear that, Coutre?"

Doctor Coutre stuck his head in the door.

"I hear, you old goat," he said. "And we're running a hospital here, not a tavern. I can't have you dropping dead under my nose. It's bad for business."

The Old Man snorted again and Doctor Coutre disappeared.

"Sit down, Germaine. Sit down. Over here."

Germaine settled himself in a chair and surveyed his father.

"You're still a tough old gull, Pa."

"Aah," the Old Man said. "I'm a tired one too."

Germaine searched into his father's eyes and he knew that it was true.

"I'm proud of you, Germaine," the Old Man said. "A flier. A Major." He folded his hands in front of him. "It is a good job, flying?"

"It's all right, Pa."

The Old Man nodded.

"Better than fishing, eh?"

Germaine shook his head.

"Oh, I don't know. I wouldn't say that."

"Sure, it is better," his father continued. "Nice clean job. Good job for a college man. Not dirty and sloppy like fishing. Any dumb bastard can go fishing."

"I never said that, Pa."

"I know. I am giving you the business a little bit."

They looked at each other for a long time.

"Pa," Germaine said, "Pa. I'm sorry about everything. All the grief."

"Grief, what grief? You have your life to live."

"I'm sorry I hurt you, Pa. I'm sorry for everything."

"There is nothing to be sorry for. You remember your Bible stories? You remember the Prodigal Son?"

Germaine nodded.

"It is true," the Old Man said. "It is all true. 'For this my son was dead and is alive again. He was lost and is found.'" The leathery face softened, the voice lowered. "'Son, thou art ever with me and all that I have is thine.'"

Germaine looked into the sunken green eyes. Doctor Coutre had been right. The Old Man's eyes *were* foxy.

"How much time do you have at home, Germaine? How much furlough? How much leave?"

Germaine braced himself.

"Ninety days, Pa."

"Ninety days. Like a jail sentence, eh?" The Old Man was smiling. "Ninety days. You could start the season with us then?"

"I don't know, Pa. I hadn't planned on that."

"You only planned on coming home and burying your father and that's all, eh? They told you to come home and bury the Old Man."

"Now, Pa. I just wanted to see you. I didn't make any plans beyond that."

"Well, now that I'm not dead," the Old Man said, "make some plans." He was staring innocently. *He didn't say anything, Germaine. But I know him like a book. He's got that foxy look in his eyes.*

"It's not as if I was asking you to take over the business, Germaine. But I have to take it easy for a while. I thought . . . you might want to help out a little bit. You know. A kind of vacation. A little work. A little play. I thought you might want to." He stared down at his hands. "It would help me out, Germaine."

Germaine lowered his head for a full minute. When he raised his eyes the Old Man was watching him.

"It would do your mother much good. And your brothers. And Reuben. I think your brother Reuben would be the happiest of all."

"Reuben?" Germaine almost laughed. "Reuben? Little Bébé? Why Reuben?"

"Well," the Old Man said, "he is the littlest. He is too young to fish in the tug and so he plays on the beach. The beach is a lonely place without a playmate. Someone a little closer to his own age, Germaine."

Germaine didn't say anything.

"I think Reuben would be so proud of his little niece. The little girl and her Uncle Reuben. Her eleven-year-old Uncle Reuben, eh?"

The Old Man was sucking in his cheeks and nodding his head.

"I would like that, my son. I would be happy. I think everybody would be happy all around."

Germaine looked at the floor again.

"That's kind of you, Pa."

"Aah, kind," the Old Man said. "Selfish. You know, your mother and I, we always wanted a little girl, Germaine. Stay with us a while."

Germaine got to his feet and moved away from the bed. Outside, the branches beat against the window. Fisherman, hear out these winds.

The birds are your brothers. There is the sky above and the waters below. This is where we all belong. Somehow we have found what was lost so long ago. A wooden hull and the hands of God holding us. Our feet are webbed. This is the way we must go. The shore arms of women and the coming of the wings, the great gulls, the burial birds. The shore voices screaming up the lake days, the gulls moving their mouths and riding above our wake. When you were born you began to die, you wait for that day now like a busted trout, the lung sacs bagging from your mouth. Staring. Waiting for the morning of the day that is next. The day with the gulls in it. The patient eternal gulls: waiting and watching and riding our wake.

Germaine moved to the bed and pressed his father's hands. Doctor Coutre came in leading Mama and little Julia.

"Daddy," the little girl said, running to him, "the big hand of the clock is on three now."

"I'm sorry, honey," Germaine said. "Grandpa and I were talking. I forgot the time."

They all stood around the Old Man. He tried to sit up as Germaine lifted up his daughter.

"This is my Daddy, honey. This is your Grandpa Le-Mere."

"Hello, little one," the Old Man said. He resisted the temptation to touch her. Children, like puppies, he knew, got gun-shy in a twinkling. "Your Daddy and I were talking about you. Would you like to stay with us for a while and live in our house?"

"By the big lake?"

"By the big lake," the Old Man said.

"I have to ask my Daddy."

"All right."

Germaine felt them looking at him. Mama. The doctor. The Old Man. Germaine looked down at his daughter. The blue eyes were alive with expectancy.

"Can we, Daddy? Can we stay in the house by the lake?"

In the face of his child, Germaine saw the face of her mother and he could hear Erika's voice. *Can we, Germaine? Can we stay in the house by the sea? Please.*

Germaine held her and looked directly at the Old Man.

"We'll stay, honey," he said quietly. "For a while . . ."

8

Old Man LeMere came home from the hospital in three weeks because he didn't want to miss Reuben's birthday and he threatened to raise a holy hell with Doctor Coutre if he did. The good doctor finally gave in but warned that the Old Man had to rest in bed and stay around the house. He talked to Mama in private. "Keep one of them locked up. Either him or the bottle."

Germaine worked with his brothers as they got the spiles all driven and the gill nets strung and the pot nets sunk. When the Old Man came home, they had started the season and were out fishing and lifting nets every other morning.

In the house by the lake it was quiet with the season underway. The Old Man fumed and tossed and tried to rest in his room upstairs. Julia came down with a spring cold and Mama kept her in the bed downstairs. And outside, only Bébé, only the boy Reuben, saw the beautiful spring being born this first weekend on the fisherman's beach.

From the shore, Reuben could watch the Old Man's fish tug floating like a bobber on the bright fish grounds a half-mile out. Under the shifting clouds of scavenger gulls, the spiles that anchored the nets seemed like match-sticks at this distance. Beyond them a slow syrupy smoke trail on the horizon would mark an ore carrier down-bound from the Lakehead to the steel mills near Chicago. Reuben wanted to work with his brothers but his father said he had to wait until he was older.

So he carried out the garbage for his mother and helped around the house and scrubbed floors, but he didn't like to stay indoors at all.

"That's a girl's work," he told his father.

The Old Man smiled, "Not when a man does it."

When Mama didn't need him to help around the house, Reuben could roam for miles up the clean dune sand that ran like a corridor between the lake and the dark rolling bluffs where the pines began. Sometimes he would cut over into the woods and then the only way you could tell that there was a Lake Michigan at all was by the noise the waves made when they thundered onto the beach below.

He usually traveled the beach first though. Particularly after a storm. The woods were fine but they never changed overnight like the beach.

One day the shore could be clean as a trout's belly. Then after a storm or a heavy blow, it would all be littered with driftwood and stringy gobs of seaweed and dead fish and sometimes pieces of nets and gear, ripped away from somebody's fish grounds and driven in by the wind.

Last year his father and brothers had even found a dead man washed ashore after a storm. He was all bloated up and didn't have any hair on his head and when they took him into town under some canvas in the truck, everybody said it must have been an old man around sixty years. But later the police from Two Rivers told his father that it was a nineteen-year-old boy who had drowned off Muskegon, Michigan a month before and had floated clear across the lake and being in the water all that time made him look old.

Afterward Reuben always thought that he might find a dead man washed in after a storm. As he poked and prowled and examined the debris in the wake of a big blow, the thought would give him a shudder; he would leap up quickly from whatever he was doing and look up and down the beach and all around him, like a startled squirrel.

He got the .22 for his twelfth birthday. He got it because of Germaine. Germaine told him that you had to be a man sometime and stop pleading and pestering for what you wanted. You had to make a straight proposition to the Old Man. At the breakfast table after Mass one Sunday morning Reuben finally stood right up to the Old Man. He stood right up and told the Old Man he wanted a rifle. The Old Man seemed surprised and looked straight through him for a long time. Then he looked at Mama and at Germaine and at everybody and then back at Reuben. Nobody said a word.

"And am I expected to buy you this weapon simply because you have a birthday coming and you expect a present anyway, so it might as well be a gun?"

"No, sir."

"Oh," the Old Man looked interested. "How then? How do you see it if not in that light?"

"I'm going to gather up shells, sir. The beach is full of them up by the lighthouse rocks, and I'm going to gather them up and sell them for ash trays."

"Oh? And have you considered the market? Who is to purchase those precious articles from you?"

Reuben hesitated and had a slow moment of uncertainty, but the wind-burned face of Germaine watching him closely reassured him. He pointed at Germaine.

"He is, sir."

The Old Man sat still for a long time, looking around at his sons. One at a time.

"And how many shells is Germaine going to buy?"

"Thirteen dollars and ninety-five cents worth, sir. Then I can pay you back for the gun. It's a Stevens. Single shot."

The Old Man looked right down the table at Mama.

"And I suppose Mama's going to buy a few thousand clamshells too?"

"Oh, no, sir. Mama doesn't smoke."

The laughter began. Quietly, like a bubbling spring, then eddied clear around the table like a strong current, and finally the Old Man's big rumble that sounded like waves breaking was the center of it all. Finally he shook his head yes, and said that under those conditions, he would be happy to do business.

The Old Man always said that he and Mama had raised four boys and they were all men who worked and ate and laughed and drank and stood right alongside him on the fisherman's beach like men. "Now," he had said, "You all have to start moving over to make more room. For Reuben." Then he started in on his poached eggs.

Reuben felt very good that Sunday morning. As he spooned up his oatmeal, he saw the Old Man wink at him once. He sat there happy, with his mouth full of cereal, and then Germaine winked at him too.

Now carrying the garbage pail out to the sandpit wasn't a chore any more. He always took the .22 with him and when he got around behind the garage, he would set the pail down for a minute and slip a bullet into the chamber so he would be ready in case he saw anything. He had to wait until he was behind the garage because then Mama couldn't see him from the kitchen window. She was always afraid for him when the gun was loaded and he didn't want her to worry.

When he reached the sandpit, before he dumped the garbage, he would fish out all the cans and bottles from the pail and set them up as targets against the far bank. Then he would crouch behind a windfall and pretend that the cans and bottles were Indians or badmen or robbers or even bears and deer.

Usually, though, the pork-and-bean cans with the red labels were Indians attacking his fort and he would have to shoot fast and reload and hold them off until help came.

He had to change his position often, of course, and keep on the move, so they wouldn't know that only one rifle was holding them off. So he would crawl and scramble the whole length of barky log pausing every few feet to snap off a shot and duck ahead to another position and shoot again and keep it up until he was sure he had created the impression that at least a dozen deadeye rangers were fighting along with him.

When all the pork-and-bean cans had been shot and torn through and sent spinning to the bottom of the sloping bank, he would hold his fire for a moment. Then rising with his gun at the ready, he would advance carefully on the fallen enemy to make sure he had got them all.

The battles and skirmishes in the sandpits slowly developed him into a very capable shot. And the skill made him restless. He began to want something more than the bottles and the cans and the pretending.

He began to want to kill something.

He decided it would be a sea gull. There were hundreds of them all up and down the beach and around by the lighthouse rocks. He could shoot one of them. Then he could throw it away or bury it and nobody would ever know.

It would have to be in the morning because then Germaine and his brothers would be out on the lake lifting the nets and there would be very little chance of anyone else seeing him because no one would be around the beach. Except Mama, of course, but she would be busy inside the house taking care of Papa upstairs and cooking dinner. She would be much too busy to be watching the beach. He made up his mind to do it Saturday morning when there was no school. At that week he hurried to the sandpit even when there was no garbage to dump. He took careful aim with every shot and didn't fire at any Indians at all.

On Saturday, his brothers were gone when Reuben got up. He washed his face and hands in the kitchen sink and as he dried himself, he could see the Old Man's fish tug out on the fishing grounds. He stayed at the table only long enough to get down a second helping of Mama's homemade coffeecake. Then he took the .22 down from the rack on the winter porch and bolted out the screen door.

The wind was blowing straight in from the lake. It slapped his bluejeans around his ankles and carried spray in high over the beach. He headed for the lighthouse rocks, past the barge spile driver beached high and dry, past the rusty twin tracks that ran down into the water for launching. Past the big sun-peeled gear shack where there were dinghies and boots and rain slickers and unmatched oars and chains and fluke anchors and slop-sided buckets of marine paints. Past all this, for nothing in the gear shack could hold him today and he went right by. He broke into a trot, his rifle at the ready, jogging all the way to the smooth green glacier rocks where the lighthouse stood. He watched the herring gulls climbing and dropping.

He threw back the bolt on the .22 and pushed a bullet into the chamber, and locked the bolt forward. He could feel his hands shaking on the stock as he picked out a gull, following it as it glided and coasted and turned in unhurried circles.

Then he jerked the trigger and the rifle moved a little and the wind carried away the noise of the shot so it sounded almost flat. The gull he had aimed at was still flying and starting to sweep away and he knew he had missed. He pulled back the bolt and the empty smoking shell spun out, end over end: he could smell the smell of burnt powder. The shot didn't seem to scare the gulls away although most of them had risen now and were twisting over the rocks like pieces of paper caught in an air current. He had loaded up and was aiming again when he heard the shout. He lowered the rifle. It was a big dark man in a blue shirt leaning out of a window in the lighthouse and hollering at him. The wind was blowing away most of what the man was saying but Reuben could hear two words very clearly.

"Goddamn you!" the man was yelling. "Goddamn you!"

Reuben stood looking at him. Then he was afraid that the man might come down and chase him. He turned and fled back to the Old Man's beach.

He ran all the way and as he crossed in front of the gear shack, the barnlike structure seemed to stand like a blockhouse. He darted in behind it and turned to stare at the ground he had covered and at the distant lighthouse. The beach was empty. There was no one chasing him. There was nothing moving at all, except a cloud of black dot around the lighthouse sky that looked like a bunch of cinders floating up from a tall smokestack. The shore had never looked so strange and alien before; he thought that he would never go up that way again. The dark man who had hollered at him was probably from the Coast Guard but he didn't have any right to swear at somebody for shooting a gull, and besides he hadn't shot it. The herring gulls didn't belong to the Coast Guard anyway. The curse the man had flung down at him from the high window slid through his conscience like a rope burn. At school, Sister Agatha always said they should say an ejaculation when they heard someone take the Lord's name in vain. Now he hunched down in a corner of the gear shack and kept saying: "Blessed be the name of Jesus," over and over again.

Very rapidly. It helped to keep the humiliation from spilling out.

He wondered if the man in the lighthouse would tell his father. He turned to stare out at the Old Man's fish tug wallowing far out among the spiles like an animal following a fence line.

It was then that he noticed the clutch of gulls bobbing slightly offshore like a string of anchored duck decoys. The sun ricocheted cleanly from their plump slick bodies making them easy to count. He counted seven of them. He pitched himself down into the square shadow of damp sand below the north wall of the gear shack and swung his rifle at the middle of the gull formation. Angrily he fired off all his resentment at the Coast Guard man and the cursing and his own stomach-sickening flight. He fired as fast as he could and reloaded and fired again.

By the time he had shot three times the group of gulls was air-borne and wheeling away so wildly down the beach that he couldn't count them and he had trouble trailing them until finally they pierced into the horizon like pinpoints and he lost them completely.

The lake rolled in, lonesome and abandoned; the only whiteness on the water now was the curling foam track. His gaze traveled a searching pathway which stretched right out to the fishing grounds. All he could see was the Old Man's fish tug still squatting far out along the fence line. Nothing more. He scrambled to his feet and after he unfolded the sand from his cuffs, he walked slowly to the house and the winter porch, feeling, in a way, a little better. But he said twenty more ejaculations nevertheless. Silently.

• • •

After dinner the Old Man announced that he was going to take a walk outside to test his legs and Mama said oh, no, he wasn't.

"Not until you're stronger, Doctor Coutre said."

"Atrophy, Mama," the Old Man said, "atrophy."

"What?"

"Atrophy," the Old Man repeated. "If I do not use my legs they will fall off. I am stronger now. Tell the doctor to put that into his pipe and smoke it."

Then the Old Man asked Reuben what he had been doing in the morning. "Nothing," Reuben lied. "Only some target practice." The Old Man said he wanted to see him shoot in the sandpit.

Mama stuffed the dinner garbage into a brown bag and his father took it and waited. Reuben reached the .22 down from the porch wall rack. He followed his father out through the screen door.

As they walked, Reuben stared down at the wide pockets that the Old Man's bird boots pushed into the sand. He remembered how hard it was for him to follow the Old Man in deep snow last winter because he sank to his crotch in the leg-long holes his father left. He would have to break a little trail for himself or get stuck like a rabbit in a snare. Except when they wore snowshoes, of course. The sturdy snowshoes could flatten out the weight of even a big man like his father and then trailing him was as easy as spearing the spawning fish in springtime.

Reuben was so lost in his memories of last winter that he walked right smack into his father's back before he realized that the Old Man had stopped and was talking to him.

"What is that, Reuben?"

Reuben thought the Old Man meant something ahead toward the sandpit. He craned to look. He couldn't see anything; he didn't know what the Old Man meant.

"I don't see anything, sir."

At that his father wheeled him about harshly and faced him down toward the beach. The heavy right arm snapped out straight over Reuben's shoulder like a signpost, aligning itself on a small naked blob of whiteness at the water fringe.

"That," the Old Man said.

Reuben squinted. It looked to be a fish, the pale underbelly bagging with water and death. It looked to be a trout or whitefish or sucker or some kind of fish. Then the water pushed in around it and moved it gently ahead and as it rolled in the backwash he could see that it wasn't a fish at all. He didn't say anything. He was so shocked he couldn't say a word.

"A gull," his father said. And Reuben knew the Old Man was right.

They walked silently to where it lay and though their shadows covered the gull like a tarp, nothing could cover the spike-round holes in the gull's neck.

"Did you kill it, Reuben?"

"I guess so," he said.

The Old Man looked straight through him all the while he was explaining and when he finished, his father studied the crumpled gull for a long time.

"You are a beach boy, Reuben. You know the herring gulls are scavengers. Yet you killed one." He stopped and shifted the brown bag which was beginning to stain. "I do not know what to say to you. If you start in killing all the garbage collectors, who will be left to collect the garbage?

Do you want to do it? Do you think you can do it? God put the gulls here to keep the lake clean but possibly God is not so smart as you are and possibly the lake would be a better lake all dirty and filthy and stinking."

"I'm sorry, sir."

The Old Man took Reuben's hand then and pressed it down hard on the dead gull's belly. The lake-cold body, the drowned feathers oozed water, frightening his fingers and sickening him.

"You must be careful about your words always, Reuben. This is the way death feels and as far as this gull is concerned, you cannot convince him of your sorrow."

Then his father told him to carry the gull up to the sheltered side of the gear shack. Reuben thought he was to bury it there and he bent to gouge a hole in the sand. But the Old Man stopped him.

"No. Just let it be. After a while the maggots will come and the flies and then the gull will go away. There is no need to bury it and hide it. A hunter should be proud of what he kills."

He wanted to be sick as the Old Man turned and struck out for the sandpit alone with the greasy brown bag. Reuben watched him dumbly. He tore his palms quickly across his thighs to blot up the revolting sticky wetness of the gull.

For days and days the gull stayed there. Reuben could see the fly-stripped carcass slipping away slowly, rotting into the ground. No one said anything about the thick decaying smell that hung over the yard until finally the rain washed heavily into the ground and it was gone. When the beach dried out only clean sand swirled over the spot and piled up at the side of the gear shack. The gull was something that Reuben wanted to forget but he knew he never would.

9

The Old Man had been right, Germaine decided. It was a kind of vacation. His uniform hung in Reuben's room, clean and pressed and put away in a storage bag and he didn't feel like a stranger any more. He wore boots and jeans and a blue workshirt and it felt good. He knew that as he got used to the hard heavy work of driving in the spiles and setting in the nets it would all be as it once was when he was a boy on the Old Man's beach. The fishermen worked the waters the way farmers work their fields and he would sweat and get hard and strong again and he would feel good. Just good.

When the nets were all in, they were ready to start the schedule of chugging out to the fish grounds every other morning to raise the nets. It had been three o'clock in the morning when Roger rolled them out of bed for the first lift of the season.

"Major," the voice rasped in Germaine's ear, "time to grab your socks." They dressed in the darkness and went downstairs in their stocking feet. In the kitchen, the Old Man was in his bathrobe, pouring fresh steaming coffee into a cluster of white mugs.

"For chrissake, Pa," Roger said. "You should be in bed."

"Bed is for a young man," the Old Man said. "A Godforsaken shell like me does not need bed."

A bell rang in Germaine's mind. *Godforsaken shell.* Somewhere, sometime, he had heard someone say those words in the same way. *Godforsaken shell.* Where? He sipped the strong coffee and watched his father carefully.

"So," the Old Man said, "back to nature, eh, Germaine? The wind and the water and the money-making lake trout. It's a long time since you fished." He pursed his lips. "Eight years ago, the summer before the war. Those days are gone. The lampreys come. The trout go. Everything changes. That is nature's plan, I think."

They urged the Old Man back to bed and then they went out and climbed into the station wagon. Ahead of them lay the long seven-mile ride through the Point Beach Forest to the quiet town where the fish tug was tied up inside the harbor.

Raphael and Gabriel climbed into the back seat and Roger started the engine. He switched on the headlights and swung the wagon back and around and onto the sand road that led to the highway.

"I think Pa should have stayed in the hospital," Raphael said.

Roger lit a cigarette and half turned his head.

"How the hell you gonna keep him in a hospital," he said. "It's a lot less grief this way."

"Cheaper too," Gabriel put in.

"Christ, it's not my idea," Roger said. "Doc Coutre says he can rest at home as well as anywhere."

"Some rest," Gabriel said. "Three o'clock in the morning and he's making coffee."

"That's the way he is," Roger said, "and what are you gonna do? Tie him down and lock his room?"

Germaine smoked and watched the yellowish road unwind between the thick, dark pines. *Godforsaken shell.* Through the heavy woods the false dawn lightened the eastern sky, and then he remembered. The past rushed out at him like water through an open floodgate and he remembered. *Godforsaken shell.* He had been seventeen when he heard those words. He slumped in his seat and half closed his eyes. Of course, they had been the Old Man's words all the time.

They had dropped Roger with his fly rod at the lower branch of the White Creek to work upstream and now Germaine and the Old Man were heading for the Upper White. The false dawn was purpling the Wisconsin countryside when Germaine spotted the huge hunchbacked object in the middle of the sand road and he coasted the battered Chevvy to a stop.

"Pa," he said. "Turtle. Lousy snapper."

The Old Man sat up.

"Is he dead?"

"Not yet," Germaine said. "Not yet he isn't." He shifted into neutral and pulled the hand brake.

The snapper lay large and dark in the headlight beams and they got out and went around to look at it closely. The turtle moved a little and left razor-like claw marks in the wet sand. Then it waited.

"Probably heading for the creek," Germaine said. "They kill trout like crazy."

They stood staring down.

"I'd run the Chevvy over him," Germaine said, "only he's too damn big."

He looked around and walked to the ditch and came back with a long finger-thick pine branch. He jabbed it into the turtle's beak and the snake-like head lashed out and struck like spring steel and the branch snapped like a stick of macaroni and it all happened fast as a match flare.

"Jesus Christ," the Old Man said.

"Bastard," Germaine said. "I'll bet he goes sixty pounds, seventy maybe."

The turtle was darting its head around now in long stretching movements.

"I think he got some branch stuck in his craw," the Old Man said.

"I'll give him something in his craw," Germaine said. "I wish to hell I'd brought the .22," he said. "The pistol."

"You going to kill him?"

"Why not?" Germaine asked. "They kill trout, don't they?"

They stood there not talking and looking down at the unmoving shell.

"I could use the lug wrench on him," Germaine said. "Only I don't think it's long enough. I don't want my hands near him."

The Old Man didn't say anything.

"You watch him, Pa. I'll go find something in the Chevvy."

Slowly, the Old Man squatted down on his haunches and smoked and stared at the turtle.

Germaine came up holding the bumper jack.

"I want to play it safe," he said. "I don't think the lug wrench is long enough." He squatted beside the Old Man. "What do you think?"

"He waits," the Old Man said. "What difference what I think?"

Germaine squinted at him.

"I can tell something's eating you. What are you thinking, Pa?"

"I am thinking this is not a brave thing."

"What?"

"This turtle. He doesn't have a chance."

Germaine hefted the bumper jack and the turtle moved ever so slightly.

"You talk like an old woman."

"I can understand this turtle's position."

"You mean he doesn't have a chance?"

The Old Man nodded.

"And that bothers you?"

"That's right," the Old Man said. "That bothers me."

"Well, of all the goddamn dumb things. What the hell do you want me to do? Get down on all fours and fight with him?"

"No," the Old Man said. "Not on all fours. Not on all fours." He looked at Germaine. "In the water. Fight this turtle in the water. That would be a brave thing, my son."

Germaine put down the bumper jack and got the thermos jug from the back seat and he didn't say anything. He drank his coffee and smoked his cigarette and he stared at the turtle and he didn't say anything.

"You're crazy," he said finally.

"It is a thought, my son. A thought. This helpless prodding old one in his Godforsaken shell like a little baby in this sand road, eh? But in the water, his home—" The Old Man snapped his fingers with the suddenness of a switch blade. "In the water he could cut down anyone, anything, any man. Fight him in the water, Germaine. Use your bumper jack in the water."

"I think you're nuts, Pa," Germaine said. "I think you're honest to God nuts."

The Old Man shrugged.

"This does not seem fair for you, eh? To be in the water with this one." He motioned at the turtle. "This seems nuts to you. Because in the water he could cripple you. Kill you. Drown you. Because in the water you are not a match."

"What the hell are you trying to prove, Pa?"

"Germaine, this turtle is putting up his life. In the road here you are not putting up anything. Not a finger or your hand or your life. Nothing. You smash him with a long steel bumper jack and he cannot get to you."

"So?"

"So. I want you to put up something also. You should have something to lose or it is no match."

Germaine looked at the Old Man and then at the turtle.

"Any fool can smash a watermelon," the Old Man said. "It does not take a brave man."

"Pa, it's only a turtle. You're making a federal case."

The Old Man looked at his son.

"All right," he said. "Do what you are going to do. I

say nothing more. Only for the next few minutes put yourself into this turtle's place. Put yourself into his shell and watch through his eyes. And try to think what he is thinking when he sees a coward coming to kill him with a long steel bumper jack."

Germaine got to his feet and ground out his cigarette.

"All right, Pa," he said. "All right. You win."

The Old Man rose from his crouch.

"No," he said. "Not me. You. You win."

The Old Man walked around in behind the snapper and gently prodded it with his boot toe and the turtle went waddling forward across the road and toppled over the sand shoulder and disappeared into the brushy growth of the creek bank. The Old Man and Germaine climbed into the car and sat looking at each other. The sun was coming up strong now and the sky was cracking open like a shell and spilling out reds and golds and blues and Germaine stared at the Old Man.

"So?" the Old Man said.

They sat for a full minute watching each other and then Germaine released the hand brake and they rolled slowly along the drying sand road and down past the huge cleansing dawn coming and the pine forest growing tall in the rising mists and the quickly quiet waters of the creek.

It was Roger's voice that brought Germaine back.

"You gonna stay with us all summer, Germ?"

It had been a long time since anyone had called him by that hated nickname. Most of his boyhood at St. Luke's parish school had been spent in fighting anyone who used it to his face. It had waved over his childhood like a banner and he had followed it into bloody battle after battle. He had actually forgotten the name until now, but as he looked sideways at Roger, he knew that Roger had not forgotten.

"For a while," he said. "A couple of months. We'll see."

"Till the Old Man dies, huh?"

He didn't have to answer the question. Gabriel, in the back seat, did it for him.

"Jesus Christ," Gabriel said.

"Well," Roger said defensively, "you gotta think about things like that."

"Maybe you gotta," Gabriel said. "I don't gotta."

They drove on in silence until they reached the highway that would take them into town and the riverside shanty where the fish tug was tied up.

Roger turned onto the highway.

"You ever hear about Ginny Dussault?" Roger asked suddenly.

"Damn right," Raphael said. "I hear plenty."

"Wise bastard," Roger said. "Who the hell's talking to you?"

Raphael snickered.

"I hear she's a good kid," he said.

"Drinks though," Gabriel said.

They laughed at Roger's anger.

"Wise bastards," he growled.

Germaine smoked his cigarette. Ginny Dussault had belonged to his boyhood. She was puppy love and a grade-school crush and the high-school prom. She belonged to the time when you believed in all the dreams and you knew damn well that you were going to live forever.

"No," he said, "I never heard about Ginny Dussault."

He hesitated, looked over at Roger. "Is she all right?"

Roger grinned broadly.

"All right? Like a mink," he said.

"Teacher," Raphael said in a shrill voice, "why is Roger still in night school?"

"He's taking a course," Gabriel said primly.

"What course?"

"The inter course."

They howled.

Roger half turned toward Germaine.

"Bastards," he said. But Germaine could tell he was not at all displeased.

Ginny Dussault. Ginny Dussault.

"I don't understand," said Raphael. "Why would a smart schoolteacher ever shack up with a dumb animal like our Roger?"

"I think she wants to improve his mind," Gabriel said.

They howled again.

Germaine ground out his cigarette as the wagon rolled into town and along the lighted deserted streets. They swung down over the river bridge and into the parking area alongside the fish shanty. Beyond the fish tug moored to the pilings, the bridge lights reflected in the moving, restless waters like a sea of pale, drowning faces—bobbing, struggling, disappearing and flowing away in the current.

Ginny Dussault, Germaine thought to himself, Ginny Dussault.

10

They spent half an hour getting the tug ready for the run out to the fish grounds. Out of the shanty gear shack came the empty fish boxes they hoped to fill by noon. Raphael and Gabriel lugged these aboard while Roger gassed up the tug and Germaine carried out the foul-weather gear. They moved quickly, quietly, anxious to have the joework over with and be underway. Once they cleared the dock, they could relax and smoke during the seven-mile run back up the coast to the nets. Now there were hundreds of pounds of ice to be put aboard and steel oil drums into which they could fling the trout guts when they cleaned them on the way back. The offal would be sold to the area farmers. It wasn't much but every little penny helped now. "Anything you get out of the lake these days," Roger said, "you keep out of the lake."

"How many gut barrels you want?" Raphael asked.

"Take two," Roger said.

"Christ, we didn't fill two all last season."

"I got a feeling it's going to be good today."

"Roger, Roger," Raphael said. He carried the second drum down to the tug.

"Jesus, what's two barrels for?" Gabriel asked as they passed.

"I dunno," Raphael said. "Maybe Roger's gonna wee-wee in one of 'em."

Roger started the engine and the twins cast off the bow and stern lines. The fish tug *Ione* backed tentatively into midstream.

As they cleared the harbor breakwater, the powerful swells of the open lake caught them full force and the stubby tug began its wallowing fight up the coast. The tug smashed ahead heavily, like an icebreaker, the waves exploding over the bow and whipping down the deck in stinging shrapnel-like bursts. Gabriel and Raphael struggled into their foul-weather gear and huddled together in the hold to smoke. Off to the eastward where the sky was reddening a little, the heaving waters to the horizon took on the shadowy cast of flowing lava. The wind was fresh and smelled of fish. Germaine squeezed into the tiny pilothouse where Roger was squinting out over the wheel. The windshield streamed with driven spray.

"Just like old times, huh?" Roger said loudly.

The tug went crashing down into a trough and Germaine had a brief gagging aftertaste of coffee. He took a deep breath as the tug labored and skidded greasily. He had shared this pilothouse with the Old Man on a thousand rolling mornings and he knew that those days were dead and gone and finished forever.

"Yeah," he said. "Just like old times."

Roger reached for a cigarette.

"About Ginny," he said.

Germaine braced himself as another rush of water boomed into them.

"We might even get married," Roger said. "I been thinkin' about it."

Germaine didn't say anything. His days with Ginny Dussault were as dead as his days with the Old Man in the pilothouse. They floated in a meaningless limbo of memory, without flesh, without blood. It was as though a stranger named Roger LeMere had said he was going to marry a stranger named Ginny Dussault. And yet Germaine felt a twinge, a pang. A feeling for what might have been when the questions were simple and the answers were simple. Once he might have married Ginny Dussault. They had grown up together and gone together and it was a habit. Like the church you went to or the paper you read or the way your family voted. They might have married then and by now they would all know what he had known all the time. He had been in the wrong nest, the wrong pew, he thought. College had started it and the war had finished it. He was a fallen-away Catholic and as Sister Justa had told him back in grade school, that was the worst kind. A fallen-away Catholic became the enemy of Holy Mother Church. Amen, Sister. Only in grade school he didn't realize the injustice of branding a baby guilty of Original Sin the moment it left the womb. In grade school he didn't realize that Holy Communion was as symbolic of cannibalism as African juju. In grade school he didn't realize that his generation of American Catholics was going to kill and be killed by a generation of German Catholics. To break with the Church was to break with his family and he had done it and stayed away.

The marriage would have been a foolish, terrible mistake.

Roger looked at him, his tongue flicking the hard sensuous lips.

"Old Man Dussault thinks it might be a good idea," he said. "He seems to be happy about the idea."

"Well, congratulations."

"Actually," Roger said, "there's no date set or anything like that. Christ, we aren't even engaged officially." He gave Germaine a sly wink. "We just go together. Coupla years now."

Germaine reached for his cigarettes and stared out at the deck. In the hold he could see the wet, slickered figures of Gabriel and Raphael huddled together. They could get in a little cat nap by the time the tug reached the fish grounds. Germaine smiled. What the hell, when you were young the questions were simple, the answers were simple, and you could cat-nap in a fish tug or a bomber or a hole in the ground. It was all the same.

"You see," Roger was saying earnestly, "this is all I know. I'm a fisherman. Just like the Old Man."

Yes and no, Germaine thought. Yes, this is all you know and yes, you are a fisherman. But like the Old Man? No, my pushy little brother, you are not like the Old Man.

There is no one like the Old Man and there will never be anyone like him again. He passes this way only once.

"The thing is," Roger said, "I'm pretty sure Old Man Dussault would like to get out of the fishing business. He's getting up there and without any sons in the family . . ." His voice trailed off and he half-turned, leaning on the wheel.

"Both Dussault boys," Roger said, "they got it at Iwo Jima. They were Marines."

"That's rough."

"Well, so there Old Man Dussault is, all alone, running his tug. There's nobody to pass on the business to."

Germaine looked at Roger, the powerful slouch, the determined eyes, the hands tight and strong on the tiny wheel.

"That's where I come in," he said. "As a son-in-law I'm right in the family. In like Flynn."

"You don't mean *buy* in?"

"Hell, no, I don't mean buy in. Where the hell would I have the money to buy in? I mean after I marry Ginny, Old Man Dussault makes me a partner in his business. That's natural, ain't it?"

Yes, Germaine thought. That's natural. Christ yes, if it was anything, it was natural.

"What about Pa?" he asked softly.

Roger looked at him harshly.

"What about Pa? I got my own life to live. He don't own me. I'm getting pretty goddamn fed up with him acting like he does. Don't pull that what about Pa stuff with me. What about Roger?" He flushed, his teeth showing white and strong like an animal at bay. "I get the picture with Pa all right. He doesn't have to hit me over the head. All these goddamn years I fish for him and do all the friggin' dirty work and break my ass for *his* business *and* what happens? Nothin' happens, that's what. He's still got me on salary. He won't make me a partner, screw him. I can run Dussault's operation. And I can *own* it."

Roger subsided as a heavy wave caught them broadside, its unleashed flowing strength slamming full into the rudder, pulling against the wheel like a waterfall. Roger's booted legs were wide stanced, braced and straining. The tug shuddered, the wave lifted them dizzily and gushed past. Roger relaxed and draped his arms over the wheel.

"Why won't Pa make you a partner?" Germaine asked.

Roger snorted and dropped his cigarette butt to the flooring.

"Why?" He turned and Germaine saw the defeated look in his eyes. "Because of you, that's why."

"Me?"

"Yeah, you. He's saving the whole shebang for you."

Germaine heard the words and he felt a genuine sorrow for Roger. Roger was trapped and he didn't deserve that.

"That's ridiculous," Germaine said.

"You goddamn right it's ridiculous. When you were here I didn't say boo, not one friggin' word about the setup because you were the number one boy and I was a punk kid. But goddamn it, Germaine. You went away and I stayed and by Christ, I've got more time on this tug than you ever had. And with all that, he still won't make me a partner. You goddamn right, it's ridiculous. I'm taking a screwing."

"I told him I didn't want it," Germaine said quietly.

"You know how he is," Roger said. "He's so goddamn hard-nosed. He believes what he wants to believe."

It was lighter now. A quarter-mile to portside the sun rays were running through the pine tops like a crown fire. With the dawn the water changed too. Around the tug, it was a clean waxy green; to the shoreward it was a hard deep blue that exploded into the white wavering line of the breakers foaming onto the yellow beach. They were off the Point Beach Forest now, the Old Man's house would be coming up soon.

"You want me to take the wheel for a while?" Germaine asked.

"All right," Roger said. "Sure. I could use some coffee."

They exchanged places. Roger got out a thermos bottle.

"You want some?"

"No, thanks."

He opened the bottle and sloshed it into the cover cup. He sipped it carefully and smacked his lips.

"Goddamn working for a living," he said. "It's a bitch."

Germaine nodded sympathetically but with the wheel in his hands and the clean wild look of this beautiful morning it actually felt like a holiday.

"It's no fun," he said.

"What I need," Roger said, "is some of that flight pay. Whattaya get? Fifty per cent of your base pay?"

"Yeah."

"And overseas pay on top of that?"

"Yeah."

"Christ," Roger stared ahead glumly, his face a dark inscrutable silhouette against the eastern sky. The throbbing of the engine filled the tiny pilothouse; the lake swished and gurgled under the hull.

"That's the whole goddamn trouble," he said. "I got nothing to show for it. Not a goddamn thing. It's the Old Man's boat. The Old Man's beach. His nets. His fish."

Germaine was watching Raphael and Gabriel. They stirred as the sunlight caught their faces. They burrowed closer to the gunwale and slept on. What were their dreams, their hopes? Did they want something more than straight salary too? Did they want to be full partners with the Old Man? Everybody a chief and nobody an Indian? Why not, what was in it for them?

The Old Man built his beach for his family, his sons, and yet it was the *Old Man's* beach. Germaine had never questioned it before but he realized now that it would be the Old Man's beach as long as the Old Man lived. He didn't know if it was right or wrong. It was simply the way the Old Man was. If Roger was concerned about title and deeds and property he would have to wait until the Old Man died. That's the way things were. That's the way the Old Man was. He sneaked a look at Roger. You're not so bad off as you think, he thought. You want title and deeds and property, wait a little. You've waited this long. Wait a little more. Be patient. The Old Man won't live forever. When he dies, the Old Man's beach will be yours. It will be yours and welcome to it. Until then, keep the death-watch. Watch and be patient.

Roger was screwing the cup back on the thermos.

"You know what I'm afraid of," he said, "is maybe it's too late already."

"Too late for what?"

"The fishing. For lake trout." Roger lighted a cigarette and leaned against the bulkhead. "You know the trout have been falling off the last coupla seasons. Nobody knew what was wrong at first but we got it pretty well pinned down now. It's the lamprey—goddamned salt-water eel from the Atlantic. They hang on the trout like bloodsuckers and kill them." The smoke came angrily from his nostrils. "And that friggin' chief of the Conservation Department says, 'Oh, no, it can't be anything like that. You commercial fishermen are just taking too many trout and we'll have to control you a little closer.' Too many trout, my ass!"

"Can't they control the lampreys?"

"I dunno. But right now all they're thinking about is controlling the commercial fishermen. That's why I said maybe it's too late already. If the trout go—" He clamped his left hand on his right biceps and brought up his arm slowly. "It won't make much difference whether I'm on this rig or on Dussault's rig. Both are gonna be worth shit."

"Now, come on," Germaine said. "It can't be that bad. This is the greatest lake-trout water in the world."

"Well, this season is gonna tell the story. If the trout don't come back this season—I dunno. We're screwed."

"The Conservation Department always seemed to know what was going on."

"Crap," Roger said. "They don't know their ass."

In the distance now, Germaine could see the spile tops that anchored their pot nets sticking up like thin fence posts. Above them, gulls were rising and falling like sail planes. He looked off to the left and there against the dark forest was the Old Man's house, proud and white above the boiling surf.

"You can head us for the nets," Roger said. "I'll get the boys up."

. . .

They were snubbed up broadside against the spiles of the pot net. A pot or pound net differed from a gill net in that it could be compared to a huge rope cage from which fine-meshed lead nets were strung like fences along the bottom. The theory was simply that fish confronted by the lead nets would follow them along seeking the end and would be channeled into the narrow funnel of the pot. As the sides of the pot rose on the spiles high out of the water, the fish couldn't swim out over the top of the trap and they couldn't swim through the cable-like mesh of the sides. They swam in a watery prison that extended from bottom to surface and very few ever retraced their entrance routes and escaped through the funnel. The simplest of funneled minnow traps operated on the same principle. Once the lead side of the pot net was lifted, the funnel was sealed and the fish inside were forced to the surface as the net rose under them like a floor. At the surface they were scooped out and flung into the hold of the fishing tug.

A gill net, on the other hand, was a less sophisticated device. This was simply bottom-weighted with lead sinkers and held relatively perpendicular in the water by cork floats along the upper edge. Fish attempting to swim through the mesh were caught and hung up by their raky gills.

Old Man LeMere fished with nets of both types. The pot nets, of course, were stationery and barring disaster their locations were not changed during the season. The gills nets offered more mobility, could be picked up easily and could be shifted if their sites were unproductive.

In the old days when Germaine had fished with the Old

Man the pot nets and the gill nets bulged and sagged with big lake trout and he remembered that the catches had run into thousands of pounds for a single lift.

Now as he watched Gabriel and Raphael crank the pot net on the hand windlasses, Germaine knew that it was a poor haul. A few dozen fish were boiling around, thrashing. They were lake trout but it was a poor haul. Germaine knew it would not weigh more than a couple of hundred pounds once the fish were gilled and gutted.

Gabriel held the net; Raphael shoveled out the fish with a long-handled scoop and dropped them into the tug's fish hold.

Roger came up to him then, shaking his head and getting out his cigarettes.

"We might as well rest and smoke," he said. "Rafe can get them."

Germaine wiped his wet hands on his woolen navy cap. He picked out a cigarette.

"Two hundred pounds," Roger said, "if we're lucky. That pays for the gas, but not for us."

They smoked and watched their brothers silently.

"What's the matter?" Germaine asked. "These waters used to be jammed with lake trout. Big big schools."

Roger nodded.

"The snakes from the sea," he said. "The goddamn snakes from the sea."

He leaned forward and yelled to Raphael who was turning with the scoop net.

"You got one, Rafe?"

"Yeah," came the answer.

"Come on," Roger said, and they clambered over to the scoop net. In the bagging depression a small lake trout was gasping out its life and as it flipped and flopped Germaine saw a dark foot-long eel streaming from the fish's underbelly. He bent closer to see and he saw that the eel was actually fastened to the fish like a leech or bloodsucker.

"That's a lamprey eel," Roger said.

Germaine shook his head in disbelief.

"They hit the trout in the open lake and then just attach themselves and bleed the fish to death."

The water washed heavily into their gunwales and the gulls wheeled over the fish ground and sat on the spile tops and the four fishermen stared down at the little scoop net.

Roger got out his small gill knife and half cut, half pried the lamprey loose from the trout. "That's the business end," he said.

Germaine saw a scar hole the size of a half-dollar rasped right into the fish's body. Fresh blood and gore were still coursing out of two nail-like holes.

"That," said Gabriel, "was caused by this." He had picked up the lamprey and had forced the sucker-like mouth open and Germaine saw the lethal rows of teeth.

"In all the years I fished with the Old Man," Germaine said, "I never saw an eel like this."

"You goddamn right you didn't," Roger said. "Because it's not fresh water. It's a salt-water eel. From the Atlantic. The Atlantic Ocean."

He nodded to Gabriel and his brother dropped the lamprey; Roger threw down the knife and pinned the eel to the deck. In an instant he had cut this way and that and the eel lay in a dozen different bloody pieces. He picked up the cuttings and flung them into the water and the gulls wheeled down from their spile tops and after the water boiled briefly the pieces were gone and the water was empty.

"It doesn't do any good," Roger said, wiping his knife. "But I feel better. They're snakes from the sea and I hate every goddamn one of them."

He lit a fresh cigarette on the stub of the old and waved his hand.

"All this water. The Great Lakes. Ontario, Erie, Huron, now Michigan and soon Superior. All this water filling up with the goddamn snakes and not a man on earth can stop them now."

They picked up their pot nets and they reset them and strung them tight and secured them. Then Germaine turned the tug southward for the Two Rivers harbor and from the wheelhouse he watched his brothers gilling and gutting out the fish in the hold and throwing the offal into an oil drum and his mind was on the scar holes in the trout bodies and the lamprey eel and its sucker-like mouth and the raspy rows of lethal teeth.

All this water, filling up with the goddamn snakes and not a man on earth can stop them now.

Germaine couldn't keep his mind off the Old Man. Michigan was always the Old Man's lake. He worked the fish grounds off this shore. He built up on this beach with his own two hands.

At the dinner meal the talk would be of fish, of the disappearing lake trout. It will be a hard season. It is not only here. All along and down the beach the talk would be the same. No fisherman is safe from the snakes from the sea. The trout fisherman will end on the beach. Some of them soon . . . this season. Ontario, Erie, Huron. This season they are farmers. They are beached. Sold out. Moved. Working in the cities.

The old days are gone. The fish are lost. This morning a few hundred pounds. The Old Man will not catch his weight in fish.

The Old Man LeMere and the lifeblood of his business going into the bellies of eels. On the deck, the brothers put away their pocket stones and knives.

The Old Man will end on the beach so very soon. There is no fighting the snakes from the sea. They will drive him high onto his own beach. They will drive him even as they drove the trout before. They will kill him, the Old Man. Even as they killed the trout.

In the pilothouse, Germaine kept the bow, like a knife, into the Two Rivers Point.

11

The Old Man invited a few of the commercial fishermen over to the house for a little beer and cards and this time they agreed to come. Smitty, Gunnar, Jacques, and Dussault. They would bring their wives on Saturday night and play a little sheepshead or hearts.

After supper Mama gave Julie her bath, then she told Reuben to go up and read her some stories. Roger and the twins were cleaning up and getting ready to go out. Germaine sat at the kitchen table with the Old Man, drinking coffee, as Mama did the dishes.

"There's a dance in Mishicot tonight," the Old Man said. "Remember when you used to go? You always took your accordion along."

"I remember," Germaine said. "It paid for the drinks."

The Old Man's eyes twinkled.

"That's for the young bucks, eh? The dancing?"

Mama swept the remaining plates from the table.

"I don't think they have nice girls there," she said. "Sitting right up at the bar."

"Ah, Mama, Mama," the Old Man said.

"Well," she said, "it's one thing for a woman to drink in her own house, but how does it look when she sits right up at the bar."

"Mama," the Old Man smiled, "in this day and age, that's how women get their own houses. First they sit right up at the bar, then they get their own house. My personal view is that this arrangement is an improvement over the ice-cream social."

"Sometimes," she said, "I worry about what they're going to bring home."

"It should be interesting," the Old Man said. He turned to Germaine and his eyes narrowed. "Old Dussault still asks about you. Every now and then. You know there was a time when he thought you might be in his family."

Germaine remembered what Roger had said about Dussault out in the fish tug.

"Yah, yah," the Old Man said, "it is not easy for Old Dussault without his sons." Old Dussault and Old LeMere, Germaine thought. One way or another the fathers lost their sons in this world. To wars. To women. To another way of life. He realized that he would have to talk to the Old Man about Roger. He would have to make the Old Man see that Roger's situation was impossible for a grown man. Heart attack or no heart attack, the Old Man had to understand that he, Germaine, was not coming back to the fishing; he didn't want the fisherman's beach or any little part of it.

"Somebody has to go to Madison," the Old Man was saying, "to explain this lamprey thing to the legislature."

"You cannot go to Madison," Mama said.

"I do not say it will be me, Mama," the Old Man said. "But it must be one of us. A fisherman must go. Someone who can talk, eh, Germaine?"

"You're right, Pa. I think somebody should go. It's the only way to get your side of the story told."

"Damn right," the Old Man said triumphantly. "Damn right."

Germaine got to his feet and took a dry towel out of the cabinet and started to help Mama with the dishes.

"Damn right," the Old Man said. "One of us has to go. This is a matter of life and death to the commercial fishermen. We have to tell the legislature that. This is not politics. This is life and death now."

Mama plunged some more dishes into the water.

"And what if the legislature does not listen?" she asked.

"What do you mean," the Old Man said, "not listen."

"What if they pass the law for the larger net sizes anyway?"

The Old Man stared at her.

"If they do that," the Old Man said, "if they do that then there will be trouble along the fisherman's beach. There will be bootleggers on the fishing grounds. They will turn honest fishermen into bootleggers and outlaws."

"You cannot fight the whole state of Wisconsin."

"You cannot fight human nature either, Mama. I know these fishermen. Smitty. Gunnar. Jacques. Dussault. And myself. When you take the bread from a man's family,

Mama, he will fight. You can drive him so far and he will not lift a finger. But when you take the bread from his family he will fight. He will fight the lampreys. He will fight the whole state of Wisconsin. And I think he would fight the Almighty God Himself."

Mama finished the dishes and Germaine wiped them and the Old Man sat watching. The twins were coming into the kitchen. They were clean-shaven and wearing suits and white shirts with ties.

"Raise a holy hell with the fishermen tonight, Pa," Gabriel said.

"I will raise a little," the Old Man said. "You too, I think."

"You know us, Pa," Raphael laughed.

"Like a book. First, Confession and then back to the tomcatting."

The twins went out and the station wagon left with a roar.

Roger came into the kitchen, pulling on his sports coat. He smelled strongly of after-shave lotion.

"You amost ready, Ma?" he asked.

She swished out the sink and dried her hands.

"I will change my dress and we can go."

They watched her leave. Roger poured himself a cup of coffee and looked at Germaine.

"Ma and I are goin' to Confession," he said. "You want to come along?"

Germaine smiled but didn't answer.

"Nothin' to confess, eh? Well, that's the way it goes sometimes."

"I don't know now," the Old Man said. "You take your mother. She goes to Confession every single week as faithfully as clockwork and the sins she has committed in her whole life you could stick under your thumbnail. It must bore the living hell out of Father Joe. It's almost a waste of gas to drive in to church."

Roger laughed and winked at Germaine.

"That's why I go along," he said. "So we get our money's worth."

When Mama and Roger were gone the Old Man was smiling at Germaine.

"He is afraid of you a little bit, our Roger."

Germaine shrugged.

"Yes. I can tell he is afraid a little bit. Good. A man should not get too comfortable. He cannot wait to take over this beach."

"Well," Germaine said, "why don't you let him?"

The Old Man looked at him calculatingly.

"Why? All right, I will tell you why. I do not trust him to run this business."

"And you would trust me?"

"Yes!"

"Pa, that's ridiculous and you know it. It's plain goddamn ridiculous."

The Old Man stiffened like some great animal at bay, his nostrils flattened, his head thrust up proudly, defiantly. Germaine flung down the dish towel and ran a hand through his hair.

"I realize I'm jumping on you, Pa, and I shouldn't because of your condition. Well, I'm sorry. But, Pa, you're using your condition like a club on me. Maybe this is the wrong time and the wrong place, but we have to have this thing out. We have to come to an understanding. You *have* to hear my side."

The Old Man exhaled in one continuing gasp.

"Well, all right," he said finally. "All right. Go ahead. Tell me. Speak!"

Germaine waved his hand and turned away for a moment. The sound of the lake surf outside filled the kitchen. He knew that if he didn't speak now, his silence would hurt Roger's position heavily. He also knew that in speaking now he was going to hurt the Old Man. There was no way around it. He took a deep breath and struggled to keep his voice soft.

"Pa, don't you see what you're doing to Roger? You say you don't trust him to run the business, but he's got the experience to run it, he wants to run it and, right now, I'd say he's running it whether you like it or not. What more do you want?"

"Roger," the Old Man said tightly, "has not settled down yet. We have discussed this many times. Roger knows what I expect from him."

"How the hell do you expect him to settle down when he doesn't even know where he stands with you? He's a grown man, Pa. You treat him like a kid on an allowance."

"Allowance!" the Old Man bellowed. "I pay him a good salary. More than he could make on any rig on the lake. I do not know what he told you, but believe me, if I paid him ten times what he gets now he would still be broke. Roger cannot handle money. When he has it, he spends it. And if he cannot manage his own affairs, I will not permit him to manage mine."

"Pa, this is his life," Germaine said quietly. "All he knows is fishing. He's a good fisherman."

"The lampreys too," the Old Man said. "They are good fishermen. It is not a simple proposition any more, this fishing. The lampreys are changing all that. It is going to take brains to beat them. Brains! Roger is strong, a good fisherman. And that is what I pay him for. But a partnership in the business? When he proves to me that he is ready, then he will have a share in the business. You think I do not want him to have a share?"

"That's what he thinks."

The Old Man snorted.

"Well, that is too bad," he said. "That is just too damn bad." His eyes flashed, his voice rose. "Let him go with Dussault then."

"You know about that?"

"Of course," he snapped. "I know all about that. When you get to be my age, angels talk to you. Well, let him go."

Reuben came bounding down the stairs then and the Old Man got up and moved into the living room.

"Julie's all ready for bed," Reuben said. "I read her four stories and she wants to kiss you good night."

Germaine went up and sat on the edge of Julia's bed. She took his hand and they stared at each other.

"Reuben read me stories," she said.

"He's a good uncle, isn't he?"

"Ummmm."

She was beginning to drowse and he kissed her forehead and turned off the lamp on the bed table. The light from the hallway fell across her face and her eyelids flickered.

"Are we going to live in Paris sometime again?"

"Yes," he said. "Sometime."

"Can he come to live with us in Paris?"

"Who?"

"Reuben. He wants to be just like you when he grows

up, so you have to show him how to fly. I promised."

She put her thumb in her mouth and he tucked the blanket under her chin and stood watching her for a long time. Then he went in to shave and clean up.

Germaine knew they were all there when he came down the stairs. He could hear the bullfrog voices carrying through the walls. Smitty. Gunnar. Jacques. Their wives were in the kitchen with Mama. When they greeted him they were cordial and kind and made a fuss about seeing him at home again. Only their eyes revealed the questions they would ask of Mama once he was gone. Woman questions that would call a spade a shovel about his child and his "wife" and the years he had been away. Mama gave him a can of beer and he realized suddenly that her answers would probably call a spade a shovel too. He smiled at them warmly and went on into the living room.

The fishermen were all sitting around the Old Man and they were all drinking beer except the Old Man, and talking. Then his father hailed him and the men jumped up and shook his hand. "Good to see you," Old Dussault said. Everyone settled down again and he noticed that Roger was sitting over on the sofa and talking with a woman. She raised her eyes and they met his. It was Ginny Dussault.

"We are all of us up against the wall," the Old Man was saying. "The way it is going we are like Green Bay flies waiting to be picked off by the gulls."

Germaine seated himself next to Old Dussault and Dussault saw him looking at Ginny.

She had aged, Germaine knew. She couldn't be thirty

yet but somehow she looked older. He was struck by her resemblance to Erika too. Blond-haired and fair and the deep haunted blue eyes. But then he knew himself well enough to realize that he looked for Erika in every woman he saw. He looked for her and he never found her and he knew that he would never find her. He turned slightly from the conversation and felt Ginny Dussault looking at him. She *did* look a little like Erika, and he had the sudden feeling that they had both died young. Erika and Ginny. In a way they were alike.

"Well, what do you think, Germaine?"

It was the Old Man's voice sharp and ringing as a bell buoy and the fishermen were looking at him.

"We present our case in Madison then?"

"Sure," Germaine said, "I think you should."

The Old Man seemed puzzled for a moment and then he slowly looked past the group and his eyes settled on Ginny Dussault. The other followed his gaze and she turned away.

"The question, Major," the Old Man said, "was can Germaine accompany his father to Madison to present the case for the fishermen?"

Germaine looked at his father.

"I will go," his father said, "if you go."

Germaine waited before he spoke. "I think," he said, finally, "that you should take Roger, Pa." He turned to the group of silent men. He had to close the door on the Old Man once and for all, in front of all the fishermen. In language they all could understand. "Roger has more experience in the tug than I ever had," he said. "If you're in the market for an airplane jockey, that's something else again."

The men smiled and nodded at his words and leaned back in their chairs. The Old Man looked at him for a long time.

"Bébé," he said slowly, "more beer for our guests."

Reuben bounded up and picked up their empty beer cans and went out to the kitchen. When he returned, he was crestfallen.

"Mama says I have to go to bed now."

"Well," the Old Man said softly, "that is the way. I did not mean to betray an ally."

"I'll get the beer," Germaine said.

He got to his feet as Bébé was saying good night to everyone.

The men were drawn up closely and listening to his father when he returned with the beer. The Old Man looked at him only briefly.

"Major," the Old Man said in the voice of a stranger, "would you please send Roger over here?" It was a dismissal and he knew that he was not expected to return and take part in the business at hand now or ever again. It was as subtle as a shift of wind but Old LeMere had resigned himself to the way things were. In that moment he wanted to reach out and comfort his father. He finished passing the beer around.

"Yes, sir," he said softly.

He went over to where Roger was sitting with Ginny Dussault. He looked down on the familiar face and suddenly her blue eyes came up and found his. Roger turned, an uncertain smile playing upon his lips.

"Well, Major," he said expansively. "You remember our long-lost brother, don't you, honey?"

Ginny Dussault's expression didn't change.

"Hello, Germaine," she said.

"Hello, Ginny," he said.

Roger was leaning forward, watching him expectantly.

"You'll hate me for this," Germaine told him, "but they want you over there." They looked over at the group of fishermen. Old Dussault was waving an arm at Roger.

"Talk, talk," Roger said. "Christ, they're like a bunch of old women. Okay." He got to his feet and patted Ginny's cheek. "Don't go away, honey." He left and Germaine felt a little awkward standing there. Ginny Dussault looked up at him.

"Mind if I sit down?" he asked.

"No."

He sat.

"Roger tells me he's an uncle now," she said.

"Yes," he said, "Roger's an uncle now."

"Well, please accept my congratulations. I didn't know you had married." He looked at her sharply but she continued right on. "And you're still flying in Europe."

He nodded.

"Yes. Still flying."

"It must be an exciting life."

"Oh, I don't know. It's a living."

He got out his cigarettes and offered her one. She took it, held it close to her lips.

"I remember how you always wanted to fly," she said. "Even in grade school. Reuben told me you're even going to teach him."

He laughed.

"Reuben's giving away military secrets." He lighted her cigarette. "How about you? What are you doing?"

"I teach school."

"Oh? Where?"

"In Two Rivers."

It was awkward. He had the feeling that they were going to wind up talking about the weather. She inhaled and looked over at the group of fishermen. He half expected to see Roger glaring at them, but Roger was holding the floor and speaking animatedly. Only Old Dussault was watching them.

"I hope," Germaine said, "that you'll forgive me for staring awhile back. I was just remembering the last time I saw you."

She looked at him full face and she really didn't look like Erika at all.

"That was a long time ago," she said.

He remembered that they had gone to the Senior Prom together in high school. He had been all over her feet because he really didn't dance very well.

"Remember the Senior Prom," he said, "how I almost crippled you that time?"

She watched him for a moment.

"I remember," she said.

She looked at him for a long time. The haunted look came back into her eyes and she shook her head. She looked like she was going to cry.

"Germaine," she said softly, "You don't know about me, do you?"

There was no way around this trouble thing in Life. A man going into trouble was like steel going into the fires and if you had the right stuff, the flames tempered you and made you strong as hell. And if you didn't have the right stuff you cracked and flawed apart and went back to the slag heap. Any way you looked at it, there was no way around it. Sooner or later, a man had to go into the flames.

And a woman too, Germaine knew.

They sat and smoked and he knew that she wanted to say something very badly and she was not saying it.

"Know what?" he asked.

"I was in an accident," she said, "an automobile accident. Five years ago."

He waited.

"I'd like a beer," she said suddenly. "Can I get you one too?"

"I can get it," he said.

"Please," she said. "Please. Let me get the beer."

"All right," he said.

She struggled to her feet and set herself and then she limped away off keel, waddling awkwardly and dragging one leg along. It was a hip injury, he knew. A bad one. Her left leg was shorter than her right. He stared at her back and then he turned away.

Old Dussault was watching him.

She came waddling, limping back and gave him the fresh can of beer. Then she pivoted slowly and stood there. She didn't look at him.

"Well," she said, "you saw?"

"Well," he said, "you've got a cute wiggle, Ginny."

She looked up sharply and he smiled at her. She looked at him for a long time.

"I had better talk to the women now," she said, "so you can talk to the men."

"All right," he said.

"I waited for you as long as I could, Germaine. I waited." She turned slowly and limped away into the kitchen.

. . .

The men were on their feet and getting their coats and jackets and they were ready to leave.

"We will take along some facts and figures," the Old Man was saying. "A little bit from everybody's books. What your lake-trout catches were the last few years and what they are now."

"Huh," Jacques snorted, "I don't need to keep books for *my* catches these days."

"I could put my trout in a five-gallon pail," Smitty said.

"We have to show them some facts and figures," the Old Man said.

"Maybe you should show them a lamprey," Gunnar said.

"These politicians wouldn't know a lamprey from a hole in the ground," Jacques said. "Ah . . . good luck down there in Madison."

"And raise a holy hell with them," Smitty said.

"We will go next week," the Old Man said. "Roger will come around to get your records and receipts before we go."

"Well, good luck," Gunnar said.

They thanked the Old Man for the beer and got their women rounded up and they all shook Germaine's hand again.

"You come and see us, Germaine," Old Dussault said. "You come see us any time."

He looked straight into Dussault's eyes.

"All right," he said.

He turned to Ginny. Roger was standing next to her.

"Good night, Ginny. It was good seeing you again," he said.

Roger put his arm around her.

"I can ride home with Dad," she said. "You don't have to bother."

"Oh," Roger said, "we'll grab a couple of beers."

Then they were gone and Germaine turned to Mama and the Old Man.

"What happened to her?" he asked.

"Ginny Dussault?" the Old Man shrugged. "She was in an accident." He went out of the kitchen and Germaine stared after him.

"It is a long story," Mama said.

"I want to know," he said.

"All right," Mama said. "It is not a secret. The whole town knows. I will tell you."

They sat down in the kitchen and Mama warmed up the coffee and he leaned forward on the chair and she told him.

He stayed in the kitchen, drinking coffee long after Mama had gone to bed. So Ginny Dussault had been in an accident. She had been with some sailor from Manitowoc and their car had smashed into a telephone pole and he had been killed.

"She was always a good girl," Mama said. "You know that, Germaine. It's hard to understand what happened. Doctor Coutre said the sailor must have been dead drunk."

He sat there for a long time, smoking and staring at the kitchen clock. The thought came to him that all the years he had been away, the little clock had been marking off the minutes, the hours, the days, the months. Outside, the fisherman's beach had been eroding and washing away in the eternal waters. And inside, the LeMere family too had been eroding and one by one they also would wash away. The Old Man, who had stood up to everything that nature threw at him for a lifetime, could not stand up to the snakes from the sea. They would beat him in the end even as they would beat Old Dussault. And Roger. And Ginny. The fisherman's life was as doomed as the lake trout. And the clock kept track of it all. How many times Mama and the Old Man must have sat in this kitchen, drinking coffee and staring at the kitchen clock.

He heard an engine outside and saw the headlight beams swinging in beside the house. Then the door opened and the soft swishing sound of the breakers filled the room and Roger came in. His handsome face was dark and twisted, his body set and braced in the doorway as though he expected the floor to pitch and roll. His deep voice smashed into Germaine's ears like a balled fist.

"I wanna talk to you, Major!"

Germaine got to his feet quickly.

"Keep it down, Roger. They're all sleep—"

"All right," Roger bellowed. "Down. Outside then. Come on."

He held the door open, waiting. He'd been drinking, Germaine knew. Just enough to be sly drunk, sneaky drunk. Germaine looked into the wild bloodshot eyes and he knew that Roger wanted to do a lot more than talk. And walking away from him now wouldn't do any good. Germaine sucked in his breath and walked quickly through the open door. He followed Roger's heavy movements down the deserted beach, the whisky smell sharp in his nose.

Roger led the way around the gear shack to the side

away from the house. He turned and leaned on the hull of the upturned dory that rested on two sawhorses for calking. His face in the moonlight had an unreal, metallic cast. Roger, the iron man. No, he didn't really want to talk. Germaine waited.

"You," Roger said, pointing a finger like a gun, "you bastard. I get the picture. Packing little Roger off to Madison for those friggin' hearings. Just so you can shack up with Ginny Dussault."

Germaine didn't say anything.

"Well," Roger screamed, "you wanna say something?"

"No. Only why don't you go in and sleep it off. We can talk tomorrow."

"Don't give me that crap. Goddammit, we'll talk about it now! There's somethin' goin' on and I'm gonna find out if I have to beat it out of you."

"What are you talking about?"

"Ginny Dussault," Roger growled, "that's what I'm talkin' about. Ginny Dussault."

"All right. What about her?"

"You tell me, buster."

"All right. I saw her tonight for the first time since high school. I understand she was in an automobile accident. And I shook hands with her."

"Bullshit. There's somethin' goin' on."

"Roger, believe me. There is nothing going on." He lighted the cigarette and looked at the hard cruel face. "You're mixing your drinks, Roger. You're jealous and you're loaded. That's what's going on. It's all in your head."

Roger's hand moved like a plunging hawk, slapping the cigarette out of Germaine's mouth.

"You don't laugh your way out of this one, buster. There's something going on all right. When I take that bitch home and she freezes up on me and I can't even touch her, I know goddamn well there's somethin' goin' on."

He took a deep breath.

"I beat it out of her and I can beat it out of you."

"You what?"

"You know what she told me, buster? You know what? She said she should have married you. Nice thing to hear from a broad you go with four years. She should have married another guy. Your brother."

"And then you hit her?"

"No, first I hit her. Then she told me."

Germaine stared at the drunken face.

"And you know it all makes sense now. Maybe that's why you came back. Maybe it wasn't the Old Man's heart at all. Maybe everybody wants to pair you up with Ginny Dussault and you'll take over the beach and everybody is happy. You'll even have a mother for that bastard kid."

"Shut up, Roger."

Roger's voice dropped like a shift of wind.

"Sure. Ginny Dussault. Pair you up. Why not?"

"You're drunk, Roger."

"Oh, she's a good lay," Roger said. "Course I don't know what kind of a mother she'd make—"

"Knock it off, Roger."

"No, no, no, she is a good lay, I oughta know."

"Knock it off, I said."

"Funny. That bothers you, huh? That I laid her."

"Shut up."

"Sweet innocent little cripple, huh? You want to hear what kind of a whore she is?"

"All right," Germaine said. "All right. She's a whore. Who made her a whore?"

Roger hit him then, full in the face, knocking him backward. Before he could regain his balance, Roger picked the dory from the sawhorses and flung it. The little boat caught Germaine in the stomach, smashing him to the ground, crushing the wind out of him. He twisted away, crawled free and there was Roger hurtling, driving him into the sand like a dropping pile driver. He was like a wild sea now, his arms rising and falling like waves, drowning Germaine in a relentless undertow of fury. His fists pounded into Germaine's face like claw hammers and came away slowly and red pinwheels burst like flares in Germaine's vision. He knew that Roger was capable of killing him now. He spun awkwardly away and struggled to his feet. He blinked rapidly, desperately trying to focus.

Roger rushed him then, and Germaine ducked, flipping him over his hips, guiding him into the ground. Again, Roger rushed and again Germaine flipped him and Roger landed, crumpled on his back. The wind was being knocked out of him and the fight too. He was not so fast getting up now, but he was still coming, his mouth half open, his breathing deep and tortured. He charged again and Germaine slammed the heel of his right hand like hatchet strokes into Roger's left arm. Then Roger bent and seized the dory oar in his right hand and, sweeping it in a wide swath, advanced steadily on Germaine, backing him against the wall of the gear shack.

The oar swung back and forth like a scythe and then Germaine ducked and it slammed into the gear-shack wall and broke off. Roger held the broken shard like a club. He lunged and Germaine side-stepped to the right and slammed the heel of his hand into Roger's neck. Roger dropped face first to the sand like a dead man. Germaine wiped the blood from his eyes with his forearm, and snuffled and blew the blood out of his nose. Then he knelt beside Roger and rolled him over and looked at him. He rubbed Roger's wrists and patted his face and watched for him to come around. For one brief moment Germaine felt that his judo chop had been too hard and Roger was dead. But then he managed to catch the pulse, and after a long while Roger's eyes flickered open and he was conscious.

"You were fighting me for the whole beach, huh?" Germaine said, "The whole goddamned beach?"

Roger's gaze was steady, his face unmoving.

"I'm no competition," Germaine said. "This isn't my beach to give, Roger, but as far as I'm concerned you can have it. This is your beach. And," he added, "Ginny Dussault is your woman. There's nothing going on."

Roger's look was that of a dead man.

"Sure," Germaine said, "you have to fight somebody."

Gently, he massaged Roger's neck. Then he stopped and extended his open right hand.

"Shake on it, Roger. All your beach?"

The expression in Roger's eyes didn't change and then his lips worked cruelly and he spat into Germaine's outstretched hand.

Germaine looked into his brother's face for an eternity and then Roger bolted upright and stumbling, staggering, he started down the long sand dune to the flattened beach. At the water's edge, he squatted like some sort of animal. He licked his wounds and cleansed himself, the blood and tears and hatred washing away in the cold biting waters of the inland sea.

12

There was blood on his pillow slip when Germaine woke up. His head throbbed and his face felt raw and pulpy. He dressed slowly and went into the bathroom and took inventory in the mirror. His eyes were blackened and his lips were swollen and pretty well chopped up. He opened his mouth and with a forefinger probed over his teeth. Then he turned on the water tap and stared at himself.

"Art thou thy brother's keeper?" he asked himself. He splashed his face gingerly.

"No," he answered evenly. "Hell, no. I am not my brother's keeper."

The water washed away the caked blood on his cheeks and shocked the cut skin. Christ. You could get killed being Roger's keeper. He dried his face carefully.

"My brother doesn't need a keeper," he addressed his reflection. "He needs a goddamn cage."

He got his Polaroid sunglasses out of the bedroom and went down to the kitchen.

His father, in a faded blue bathrobe, was standing at the stove pouring out a cup of coffee. Germaine tried to sound casual. "Good morning, Pa," he said.

The Old Man turned, with the coffeepot in his hand.

"Good morning," he said finally.

The Old Man handed him the cup of coffee and poured another.

"They're all at church," he said. He motioned to the table and they sat down facing each other.

"Julie too?"

"She wanted to go along. That's all right, isn't it?"

"Sure. I guess so."

"Ah, it makes your mother happy."

"Sure."

The Old Man blew on his coffee.

"Anything happen last night? You and Roger get into it?"

"Oh, we had a little talk."

The Old Man nodded.

"He is a great one for conversation, our Roger." He ran a palm over his mouth. "That is just the kind of man to have down in Madison with the lawmakers. A talker."

Germaine felt no resentment for Roger. He lit a cigarette and forced his puffy lips into a smile.

"It was a misunderstanding, Pa."

"Sure. A misunderstanding. And so now you are wearing dark glasses."

Germaine dragged on the cigarette, its bulk large

and unfamiliar, almost cigar-like between his lips. He shrugged, remembering Roger's face in the moonlight.

"I think we got it all straightened out last night," he said.

The Old Man was skeptical. He swallowed some coffee and worked his lips.

"Well," he said, "last night was last night. I think it got all snarled up again this morning."

Germaine shot him a look that did not escape the Old Man.

"Ginny Dussault," the Old Man said. "She called on the telephone a little while ago. Ginny Dussault. She is on her way over here."

"Here? Why?"

"Perhaps she wants to see how you look in dark glasses." The Old Man hunched forward expectantly. "That is what you two were fighting about last night?"

"Pa," Germaine protested, "we really weren't fighting."

"A technicality," the Old Man said, pointing his forefinger at Germaine's face. "You were not fighting. He was fighting. About Ginny Dussault?"

Germaine lowered his head and rubbed his aching temples.

"It's a mixup, Pa. Roger just didn't understand."

The Old Man was nodding his head.

"It is a mixup, I grant. But Roger understands all right. You are the one who does not understand. It is not our Roger that Ginny Dussault is in love with."

Germaine raised his head slowly, his eyes seeking the Old Man's.

"Yes, Major. The situation has interesting possibilities, no?"

"She's coming over here?"

The Old Man grunted and fiddled with his cup.

"You know," he said, "you disappointed me last night. I did not think that you would do that to me."

"You mean about Madison?"

"Yes. About Madison."

Germaine reached over and touched his father's rough hand.

"I'm sorry, Pa. I thought we got all that straightened out before."

The Old Man was resigned. "You will not go to Madison then?"

"No." He patted his father's arm. "Roger is your man, Pa. He'll fight for this beach. He'll fight like hell."

The Old Man sighed and rubbed his nose.

"Well," he said. "Well. More coffee?"

"I'll get it, Pa."

He went over to the stove and got the pot. He filled the cups and watched his father—the Old Man was blinking a little. He put the pot back and sat down and smiled.

"Pa, I've been thinking. Maybe it would be better if—for you and Roger and everybody if . . ." he ran a hand over his forehead.

"If you went away?"

"Yes."

"There is no need to go away. It was my hope that you would come back to the fishing, Germaine. I thought that, after all, your life was here on this beach. I was wrong, it seems. Wrong. But there is no need to go away."

"I think it would be better for Roger, Pa."

The Old Man snorted. "Roger again. Germaine, if you

go away I will not be here to see you again. You know that."

He nodded and pulled on his cigarette. He had his father backed into a corner now. The great hulking frame waited, the sharp old fighter's eyes watched for his next move. What the hell, Germaine decided. This was the time to settle it for Roger once and for all. He took a breath and made his move.

"All right, Pa. I'll stay. We'll stay as long as we can. *If* you tell Roger that this is his beach. Once and for all. Today. Make him a full partner."

The Old Man squinted at him, his lips set.

"Otherwise you leave."

"Yes."

"You put a price on love, Germaine?"

"Not on love, Pa. On peace."

"You are hitting an old man. Hard."

"I know it," he said softly. "But it's the only way, Pa."

"Yah. Yah. Change. Everything changes." He shrugged. "All right, I will tell Roger. What the hell."

"What the hell," Germaine said.

They heard a car engine then and the Old Man turned, his huge head held high and alert, like a bird dog testing the wind. He turned back, his brows raised.

"So," he said. "So you are home for a visit." He got to his feet as the green pickup truck swirled into the driveway.

"Well," he smiled, "another client. It has been nice doing business with you, Major."

Ginny Dussault was on the porch and the Old Man went over and opened the door.

"Come in, Ginny. Come in."

She was wearing levis and a lumberjack shirt. She seemed out of breath and her face was flushed.

"Good morning. I hope you don't think I'm foolish—" She saw Germaine then and stopped, her eyes large.

The Old Man pursed his lips.

"Forgive me for not being dressed," the Old Man said. "We were just having coffee."

She nodded, her eyes on Germaine's face.

"Would you like some coffee?" the Old Man asked.

"No, thank you."

"Well," he said, "If you will excuse me then, I will go up and get some clothes on."

He left, pulling the hall door closed behind him. They listened to his clumping footsteps through the wall. In the quiet they watched each other.

"I'm sorry, Germaine."

"That's all right. It wasn't your fault."

She bit her lip.

"It was a misunderstanding," he said.

"When Roger's like that, he has a terrible temper. I just couldn't control him."

He laughed. "Neither could I. But don't worry about it. It's all straightened out."

Her eyes were frightened and unbelieving.

"Can we go somewhere and talk, Germaine?"

"Sure. The living room. The porch. Outside?"

She shook her head. "Can we go for a drive?"

She was afraid of Roger. Of Roger coming back from church and seeing them together. It was understandable. He swallowed the coffee and carried the cup to the sink.

"All right," he said. "For a drive."

. . .

They didn't talk as Ginny guided the battered pickup truck over the twisting sand roads of the Point Beach forest. He smoked and slumped in the warm sun and watched the dark pine trees moving by.

"No church on Sunday?" he asked.

"Six o'clock Mass," she said. "I go alone."

They came out of the woods then and the clean beach sand ran lonely and beautiful for miles. The wind was fresh and sweet and the big blue lake glistened and rolled smoothly into the concrete jetties.

"Would it be all right if we went over to Molash Creek? Where it comes into the lake?"

He grunted.

"All right."

"It's so beautiful there. I used to go there all the time when I was a little girl. I used to run over those dunes and go wading—" She broke off and they drove a while in silence.

"Molash is fine," he said.

They walked along the creek bank without looking at each other and then she took his hand.

"Germaine," she said, "I'm sorry."

"Don't be," he said. "It's all right."

"I mean I'm sorry about everything—" her voice broke and she stopped walking.

"I've made a mess of my whole life, Germaine. I'm scared."

He looked at her then and saw the wetness on her cheek, the trembling of her lips.

"Let's have a cigarette," he said.

They sat in the sand at the edge of the creek and smoked and he watched her carefully. She was staring out over the water.

"What are you afraid of, Ginny? I mean, besides Roger."

She didn't answer right away.

"I'm all right now," she said finally. "I shouldn't be telling you my troubles."

"What are you afraid of?" he repeated.

She looked at him for a long time. "I'm afraid of what I'm becoming," she said finally. "An old-maid schoolteacher."

She bent her head and the crow's-feet around her eyes deepened and spread. She was trying not to cry.

"I'm getting old," she said. "That's what I'm really afraid of. I'm getting old and I don't have anything to show for it."

He cupped the cigarette and dragged on it slowly. She was saying the same thing Roger had said out in the fish tug. *That's the whole goddamn trouble,* Roger had said. *I got nothing to show for it. Not a goddamn thing.* What did it have to be? A marriage? A house? Money in the bank? Kids? It had to be happiness, he knew. One way or another it had to be a little happiness. A little love. If you didn't have that to show for it, the rest weren't worth a damn.

"You're young yet," he said. "You don't have anything to worry about."

She turned and looked at him. Her eyes were misty.

"I'm all right now."

"Sure you are."

She moved suddenly and buried her face against his chest and cried.

"It's such a mess," she sobbed. "Such a mess."

He smoked and patted her shoulder but his thoughts were of the Old Man. Of a new grave, and the slow tired voice of Father Joe talking to the friends and survivors of George LeMere. The huge body still. The flashing eyes closed. The booming voice silenced; the great Spirit gone. Finished. Gone. The Old Man going into the ground.

The great geese flights would come rolling and billowing over the lake country like clouds. The wind would be out of Canada for weeks on end. The whitecaps would sweep across the fish grounds lonesome and abandoned and empty. Empty. This will be empty beach hereabouts, Old Man. Clear back to the dunes.

"It's everything," Ginny Dussault said. "Isn't it?"

"Yes. Everything."

It was a lot of things that had to do with the years and years of being away from the Old Man and then one day he was dead and all the years were dead and it was too late for anything. He trembled involuntarily and he knew that he was feeling the very same way he had felt years and years ago when he lay shivering in his bed, listening to the wild winds and praying to God to let his father live forever.

"It's guilt," she said. "That's a bad feeling."

"Yes."

"I know about guilt," she said. "I wasn't punished for that boy's death and I wanted to be punished. But I didn't have the courage to kill myself. I guess that explains why I let Roger own me. I think this is a pretty old story with people."

"Yes," he said, "an old story."

She raised her eyes to his.

"I read somewhere that every good woman is part whore. Part saint, part whore. And neither part is worth much without the other. Do you believe that?"

"Sure," he said, "I believe that."

She kissed him then, her eyes open, her cheeks wet.

"That's just for listening," she said. "Thank you."

He flipped the cigarette butt into the creek and pulled her to her feet.

"You'll be all right," he smiled.

They walked back to the truck and he opened the door for her.

"Is it too late for us, Germaine?"

"For *us*?"

"Yes."

"Is that what you want, Ginny? Us?"

"Yes. I always have. You knew it."

He put his arms around her and she kissed him again. Her face was still wet but this time her eyes were closed.

13

The Old Man and Roger left for Madison that afternoon.

Germaine clasped his father's hand and waited for the Old Man to speak but he didn't.

"Take care, Pa."

Old LeMere nodded.

Germaine walked around to the driver's side and reached his hand into the wagon.

"Good luck, Roger," he said.

Roger's eyes laughed at him, his hands firm on the wheel.

"The same to you, Major," he said quietly.

Then they were gone, swallowed up in the dark green forest and everybody stood there watching down the empty road. Mama was holding a hand to her mouth.

"A foolish thing," she said. "To go in his condition."

Germaine put an arm around her waist and led her back to the house.

"He'll be okay, Ma."

After they helped with the dishes, the twins sprawled around the living room reading the Sunday *Milwaukee Journal.* Julia cuddled up next to Reuben and he read the comics to her. Germaine sat down with his mother at the kitchen table.

"Don't worry yourself, Ma," he said. "It'll be all right."

They drank their coffee and Mama shook her head.

"He's the stubbornest man in the whole world," she said, "your father."

"It's a good thing his sons don't take after him."

Mama smiled and her face softened.

"And every one of you just as bullheaded as he is."

"You have to fight fire with fire, Mama."

She brushed a damp wisp of hair from her forehead.

"What good can it do to go to Madison? Why should they listen to a fisherman?"

"They will listen, Mama. It's a public hearing."

"Then they can go right ahead and pass their law anyway."

Germaine smiled.

"Maybe. But that's the way it's done. That's democracy."

She shook her head.

"A wild-goose chase," she said. "That's what it is for your father."

He got out a cigarette.

"I wouldn't bet against him, Mama. At least they'll know the score down there when he's done talking. The fishermen couldn't find a better spokesman if they hired one."

She sipped her coffee and then stared at him.

"You didn't want to go with him?"

"It's not that, Mama," he said softly. "I *couldn't* go with him. Roger has to be the one."

She nodded her head in agreement.

"Yes," she sighed, "he had to be the one. And the pity is, he'll never thank you for it."

"It's no pity, Ma. I don't want him to thank me. I just want him to have his chance."

They sat without talking, listening to Reuben's voice coming from the living room.

"And what about Ginny?" his mother asked finally.

"What about her?"

"Well, you know what I mean. Roger is no good for her."

He inhaled deeply.

"That's none of my business, Ma."

"I think," she said firmly, "that Roger made it your business last night." He shrugged. "That girl never got over you, Germaine. Not deep down inside. She'd marry you in a minute."

He shook his head at her. "Mama, Mama."

Her tone sharpened. "Well, why not? She would, and *you* know it."

"It just occurred to me," he smiled, "that the men aren't the only stubborn ones in this clan."

His mother ignored the remark. "She would make a good wife. *And* a good mother."

"For a Catholic," he said.

She didn't ignore that one.

"*That,*" she said, "is something for you to work out. But you know as well as I do that Julie should have a mother raising her."

He toyed with his cup, then drained it.

"You're serious about this whole thing, aren't you?"

"Of course I'm serious," she said. "Ginny Dussault is a good woman. You know, you're to blame for a lot of this, Germaine. She trusted you and you broke her heart. I told your father that even before the accident. You owe that girl something, Germaine. You owe her part of a lifetime."

He stared into his empty cup and she rose and brought the pot over.

"That's really the reason you stayed away," she said, "isn't it?"

He watched the black liquid flowing into the cup.

"No, Ma," he said softly. "It was because of a lot of things."

"But Ginny was *one* reason, wasn't she?"

"Yes. She was one reason. But not the real reason."

She returned to her chair and refilled her cup.

"I think you deceive yourself, Germaine. She was the real reason."

He reached for the cream and didn't say anything.

"Your father thinks that's why you left the Church. To justify what you did to Ginny. You put yourself in a position to say, well, how can a good Catholic girl marry an ex-Catholic? She can't. And so you've justified your position and Ginny Dussault isn't your business any more." She paused and searched his face. "Only she still is. And I think you know it."

He concentrated on his cigarette, annoyed now at the turn of the conversation. It was irritating to be lectured like this. It was as though his mother was talking to Bébé, telling him to eat his spinach or wash behind his ears. What really annoyed him was the tone—the mother-knows-best-dear tone that demanded unswerving, blind obedience and permitted no deviation. He drew on his cigarette and the quick flush of anger passed. Deep down in her heart, a mother probably always regarded a son as some sort of incompetent idiot, he thought. He could command men or fly a million-dollar aircraft or even change the course of history. But to dear old mom, a son would always be a helpless bonehead who at best could only bumble through life without her steadying, clear-visioned, selfless guidance. Germaine almost wanted to tell his mother that she would make one hell of a bomber pilot. But he held his tongue.

"Mama," he said, "the Jews have a phrase for all this."

His comment took her by surprise.

"What? What did you say?"

"I said the Jews have a phrase for it. The Jews say 'don't mix in.' "

"Don't mix in? You mean *butt* in?"

"That's what they mean. I guess it could apply to Christians too. Especially Catholic-type Christians."

She looked pained, her body stiffened.

"All right," she said. "That's the way you feel—I'm butting in? I'm only trying to help, Germaine."

"Mama, Mama," he said tenderly. "I know. I know you are. But the way you're talking about this thing—it's like getting ready for a shotgun wedding."

"All right," she said. "If you think it's funny, there's no use talking about it."

"Don't be angry, Ma."

She sat immobile, her lips tight.

"I'm sorry," he said. "I don't mean to give you a lot of sass, Ma. But you're—you're pushing pretty hard, Ma."

She sipped at her coffee and then put a hand to her cheek.

"I won't say anything more," she said.

"Ginny Dussault is a fine woman, and this is all an interesting idea. But," he finished weakly, "we shouldn't mix in."

"I won't say anything more," she repeated.

He went over then and put an arm around her and kissed her cheek.

"We're still friends," he said, "aren't we?"

She nodded, and looked up. Her eyes were troubled.

"Talk to her, Germaine," she said. "It can't hurt anything to talk."

He patted her shoulder and didn't say anything.

They were stretched out on the beach in their swimming trunks. Flanked by the twins, Germaine rested on his elbows, smoked and watched Julie and Reuben digging in the sand at the water's edge. Without the wind, he thought, the sun would burn out a man's brain on this open beach. But the fresh, constant breeze off the lake washed over them like cool water. He wriggled his toes into the damp sand and relaxed.

"Hey, man," Gabriel said, opening one eye, "I wonder what the poor people are doing today."

"They're lying in the sun," Raphael said. "Because it's Sunday and they got the day off."

Germaine watched the children bent over and squatting, their heads almost touching. He bet himself that Reuben would scoop out a reservoir dam and fill it with lake water and that his biggest engineering feat of the day would be keeping Julie from dynamiting things prematurely.

Reuben's words came floating up the shore like windblown leaves.

"No, no, Julie. Don't dig there. Dig here."

A drop of perspiration ran down Germaine's nose and he removed his sunglasses and wiped his face with the towel. Gabriel was looking at him unbelievingly.

"Man," he said, "that looks like a bunch of spoiled hamburger."

Raphael whistled.

"Roger did all that?"

Germaine replaced the glasses and smiled pleasantly.

"I bruise easily," he said.

"What was the beef?" Gabriel asked. "About Ginny Dussault?" He waited for a reply and when none came he shook his head. "Boy. Two brothers, their own flesh and blood, fighting over a broad. Excuse me, Germaine. I mean, a woman."

Germaine rested his chin in his palm and listened.

"That's something we haven't done, Rafe. Fight over a broad."

Raphael grunted. "I've seen your women," he said. "I wouldn't raise a finger."

Down at the lake edge, Reuben was filling a pail with water.

"What are you going to do after you finish high school?"

"Who," Gabriel asked, "me?"

"Both of you," Germaine said.

"The Corps, man. Uncle Sam wants us. You got any pull? Use your influence."

"The flyboys got a cute uniform," Raphael said. "Make us an offer, Major."

"The navy might be okay," Gabriel said. "But they stick all the swabbies in those tight pants."

"And he's built funny," Raphael said.

"What this country needs is more pockets for the navy."

They stopped and looked at Germaine innocently.

"That's a great routine," he said. "It should kill them down at the draft board." He rolled over onto his back. "Keep an eye on the kids, will you?"

"Yes, sir, Major, sir," Gabriel snapped.

"Two bandits," Raphael said, "at six o'clock."

They reminded him of the young bushy-tailed crewmen of the old 8th Air Force who had taken the Fortresses deep into Germany on the suicidal daylight raids. Thirty and forty planes were lost out of every mission in those days. Three hundred, four hundred crewmen. Baby-faced kids who looked as if they didn't have a serious thought in their heads. But they ran the radios and worked the guns and plotted the courses and died over Germany like flies. The survivors grew older and cautious and clannish and gun-shy.

"We were born in the States," a drunken bombardier had told him one night in London, "but we all grew up overseas."

The older ones had watched quietly as the eternal replacements flowed into the battered squadrons like plasma—baby-faced kids, bright-eyed and bushy-tailed, wise-cracking and eager.

"Why don't you go to college first?" he said.

"Greato," Gabriel said. "Rah rah."

"Get yourself an education first. Then if you still have to go into service, it'll be a better deal for you."

Gabriel brightened. "Officer material, hey, Maj?"

"Well, yes."

"Big deal."

"We could puncture our eardrums and be 4-F," Raphael said.

"Puncture your head," Gabriel snorted.

Germaine took one last drag from the cigarette, field-stripped and flung the compressed wad into the wind.

"You should be thinking about doing something," he said. "You're not kids any more."

"So, what's to do?" Gabriel said. "Maybe we should bum around the world. Like *you* did."

He ignored the sarcasm.

"You'll have to make your way pretty soon. The Old Man won't be able to help you. You ought to be thinking about that."

"Who the hell wants to be a fisherman anyway?"

The Old Man, he thought. The Old Man wants to be a fisherman. He wanted to go to his grave being a fisherman and now God won't let him. God and the lampreys.

"Does the Old Man want you to go to college?"

"He never said," Gabriel answered. "I don't think so. I think he always figured we'd stay and work for him."

"You know that's going to be out now."

"Yeah," Raphael said, a little sadly. "That's gonna be out, for damn sure."

Germaine shook another cigarette from the plastic pack and turned the lighter on his palm.

"I'm not going to wet-nurse you," he said, "but you have to face up to a couple of hard facts."

They looked at each other and remained silent. Gabriel traced a pattern in the sand with his forefinger.

"Number one," Germaine said, "the fishing business is shot as far as your future goes. I mean working for Pa—or *with* him. Number two, I don't think Pa is going to live much longer. And number three, do you want to wind up like Roger?"

They looked up at him in sharp surprise.

"I only mention Roger as an example. He didn't want college. He ducked the army. He trained himself to be a fisherman, to take over from the Old Man, and God knows he's qualified but now he's *not fitted* for anything else but fishing. When the fishing goes bust it'll be as hard on Roger as on the Old Man." He stopped at the realization of what he had just said. *As hard on Roger as on the Old Man.* He had always regarded himself as more like the Old Man than Roger was, but now Germaine saw that it wasn't true. It simply wasn't true. Roger was like the Old Man. Roger had followed in his father's footsteps. Roger had dedicated his life to being like the Old Man. Suddenly, Germaine saw the truth that had remained hidden from him all these years. Roger had become the Number One son in the Old Man's heart long ago. Who else was there to share the Old Man's love for this stretch of sand? Mama? The twins? Bébé? No. Only Roger. Of course. The knowledge left him feeling like a stranger in an alien place. He had been stupid not to see it. It wasn't all for money that Roger had stayed. What the hell. He couldn't have been making any all these years. He stayed because he *wanted* to stay. The Old Man knew it.

Germaine felt like a fool. He had misjudged his father badly. The Old Man was really closer to Roger than to anybody else. Mama. Doctor Coutre. Father Joe. What the hell did they know about what was in the Old Man's heart? "Take over the beach, Germaine." "There's no one else, Germaine." He shook his head at his stupidity. And he had threatened his father to make Roger Number One boy or else. Roger the heir apparent. It was laughable. Germaine wondered what would have happened if he had taken up the Old Man's proposal and returned to the beach. They probably would have drowned me, he thought. No, he reconsidered. No. They probably would have let me run things and never said a damn word. The LeMeres had a strange kind of loyalty. And love too, he knew. And love too.

"I've got some money saved," he said. "If you want to go to college, I'd like to help you. Both of you."

"You don't owe us anything, Germaine," Gabriel said. There was no sarcasm in his voice now. Actually, Germaine detected a warmth, a directness that he had never noticed before.

Raphael nodded in agreement.

"Like Gabe says. You don't owe us anything . . ."

"Oh, yes, I do," he said. "Yes. I do."

"What about Marquette?" Gabriel asked. "Or Notre Dame? You want your hard-earned money goin' to the mackerel snappers?"

Germaine laughed.

"Some of my best friends are Catholics," he said. "You name it. And if you can get in I'll help with the freight. Deal?"

"That's a lot of money, Germaine," Gabriel said earnestly. "Two of us in school at one time."

"I've got a rich uncle," he said. "But look, don't plan on hiring secretaries or anything. And some work won't kill you. Meal jobs at the very least. But I'll help as long as you're worth it. You goof off and the money stops. We'll have a simple deal."

"This is nice of you, Germaine," Gabriel said. "Honest to God. It's—it's nice."

"Deal?"

They nodded.

"All right." He stuck out his hand and they put their right hands on it.

"Deal," they said solemnly.

"All right, men," he said. "Now let's go out and win one for the Irish."

He got to his feet, took off his sunglasses, kicked off the sandals and sprinted down the beach.

"Last one in is a Catholic," he flung back at them.

They caught up with him at the water's edge and their bodies all shot into the clean blue water together. On the beach, Reuben and Julie crouched expectantly, the eyes wide open and excited, like frightened little squirrels.

They surfaced and stood in the rolling neck-deep waves, laughing like idiots, the ice-cold water already turning their bodies to goose flesh. Then Germaine saw her, Mama, coming down the beach and calling to them.

"Germaine, telephone, Germaine."

"Maybe it's Marquette," Gabriel said.

"Or Notre Dame," Raphael said.

"Ginny Dussault," his mother called. "It's Ginny Dussault."

14

The drive down to Port Jefferson was beautiful. A full moon hung over the quiet lake like a star shell as they rolled down the highway past the dark shadow jetties and the rock-strewn beaches.

They drove without talking, the music on the radio turned down low.

"You don't think this is foolish," she said, "do you?"

"Going to the Fish Shanty? No. The Smiths put out a fine dinner."

"I mean just going out," she said. "The two of us." He saw her half-turn toward him, her face anxious in the dash light. "Your mother thought it would be all right."

He recalled his conversation with Mama that afternoon. Christ. His mother should join the Grey Ladies or the USO or something.

"Mama knows best," he said, "and I don't think Roger would hit an old lady, do you?"

She laughed nervously.

"I thought I was in love with him. I really did. But I was just rationalizing. Does that make me a whore?"

He reached out and touched her cheek. She held his hand.

"No," he said. "Hell no, Ginny. We can't go back but the past is past and to hell with it. We can start fresh, if that's what you want."

"Is it what you want?"

"I think so," he said. "Yes. Why not?"

She stared at him for a long time.

"I'll give up the Church for you, Germaine. Do you want me to?"

"It doesn't make any difference."

"I'll give it up," she said. "Then we'll both be beyond the pale."

"I have the feeling," he said, "Father Joe will be happy to see me leave town."

"You don't have to marry me, Germaine," she said softly. "You don't have to."

He reached his arm around her shoulder and drew her close.

They sat in a corner of the dark dining room, having their drinks and waiting for dinner. Germaine leaned back in the solid captain's chair and surveyed the half-filled room. Red and green ship's running lights dotted the shadowy walls. Delicate, fine-meshed gill nets hung in lighted glass cases and huge mounted lake trout clung to the walls like a silent school of fish. In the middle of the room, a cook bustled around in the open charcoal-hearth area broiling fish steaks.

"This is the way to make money in the fishing business," he said. "With a dining room and a liquor license. Maybe this is what the Old Man should have done."

"The LeMere Brothers Fish Shanty?" she smiled.

"LeMere and Son," he corrected. "Maybe if he had branched out in the old days, he could have been in the restaurant business too. That would be a nice cushion now. What the hell. You don't have to catch all your own fish. You can buy through a broker and let somebody else worry about the lampreys."

"I can't see George LeMere in a kitchen," she said.

"I think he couldn't see it either," he said. "Well, we can't all be businessmen."

Through the window, he saw the moonlight glistening on the little inlet that ran behind the parking lot. Moored to the shore was one of the squat white little gillers that belonged to the Smith Brothers.

"Do you know any of the Smiths?" he asked.

She shook her head.

"No."

"They're quite a family," he said. "Quite a bunch. I think the whole family tree is hooked up with the business in one way or another."

"It's a nice place to visit," she smiled. "But I wouldn't want to live here."

The waitress brought their salads.

"Is Evelyn Smith around?" he asked.

"I think so, sir. She was in the kitchen a little while ago. Do you want me to get her for you?"

"No," he said. "No, thank you. I'll see her later."

The girl smiled and left.

"Old flame?" Ginny asked.

"Old friend," he said. "Evelyn Smith is the prime mover behind this organization. Everybody in Port Jefferson will tell you that."

"Including the Smiths?"

He smiled.

"Including the Smiths," he said. "If she was a man, she'd be running the whole state. Or the whole damn country. Remarkable woman."

Ginny sipped her Manhattan.

"Already I don't like her."

"You have to give credit where credit is due."

"You have to," she said. "I don't have to. She probably looks like a movie star too."

She looked at him, her eyes sparkling. "Are you going to propose to me?"

"No," he said. "I'm not asking you. I'm telling you. We're going to get married."

"That's good," she said. "I never put much stock in proposals." She reached her hand to his. "It almost makes up for everything, doesn't it, Germaine?"

"Sure," he said. "Sure it does."

He patted her hand.

"I'll be a good wife, Germaine."

"Promises, promises," he said. "That's all I get from you."

"What if we had gotten married way back there," she said. "It wouldn't have worked out, would it?"

"I think we'd be divorced by now," he agreed.

"We just aren't the same people any more, are we?"

"No."

"We're good for each other now, aren't we?"

"Yes, I think so."

She sighed, her face radiant in the soft light.

"I'm lucky, Germaine, very, very lucky."

"Damn right," he said. "It was either me or the convent."

She laughed quietly.

"Are they going to be surprised when you bring me back?"

"Who, the Old Man and Mama?"

"No, your friends in Paris."

"Oh, I suppose a few heartbroken mademoiselles will decide to end it all in the Seine. Just a few."

"They might as well," she said. "And if they don't jump, they get pushed. A Dussault is as French as they are. They don't come any Frenchier."

He watched her eyes, her wet lips pursed and determined.

"I'm pretty lucky too," he admitted.

"Certainly," she said. "*Beaucoup.*"

The tall, well-groomed woman smiled as she neared their table.

"Germaine," she said warmly, her arms outstretched.

He took her hands and kissed her cheek.

"Evelyn," he said. "Evelyn."

He introduced her to Ginny and they sat down.

"Well," Evelyn Smith said, "this is a pleasant surprise. Or did you just want to complain about the service?" Her eyes moved over his uniform and rested on his sunglasses.

She turned to Ginny.

"I thought the flyboys only looked that way in the movies."

"They have to wear them," Ginny said. "They all have bedroom eyes."

The older woman smiled.

"Well, what brings you down to earth? Discharge?"

"No," he said, "a visit. Just a visit."

"Your people are still fishing, aren't they?"

"Yes," he said. "Yours too, I see."

She waved a strong hand. "I don't know for how long," she said. "We're beginning to buy most of our trout from Canada. Can you imagine that. Canadian trout? You know about the lake trout, don't you?"

He nodded.

"The Old Man went down to Madison today for the hearing."

"Well, I wish him luck. But I don't think anything's going to come of that. They can stand up down there and yell about this and put the blame on that, but that's not going to fix up the fishing. If we didn't have the restaurant, I think we'd sell out. It's a rough business now, Germaine." She looked at him earnestly, her voice low. "Your father say anything about getting out?"

"He's from the old school," he said. "He'll go down with the ship."

She shook her head.

"He won't be the only one," she said. "I wish him luck. Well," she brightened, "that's enough shoptalk. I didn't mean to ruin your evening. So, otherwise how's the family?"

"Fine," he said. "Fine. And yours? Lincoln? And the kids? Little Al and Lloyd?"

"Whoa," she said, "you've been away. Little Al isn't so little any more. He's down at college. Beloit. Lloyd will go as soon as he finishes high school."

"That's good," he said. "Good."

"Well," she smiled, "it's good and expensive. But we'll get it out when they come back. I forgot to tell you that the restaurant business is getting pretty rough too. Cooking, I can do. Brains I have to buy."

A waitress appeared at her shoulder, smiled apologetically and whispered to her.

"Duty calls," Evelyn Smith said. "I'm sorry but I must leave. Ten to one, somebody found a fishbone in the French fries."

Germaine got to his feet and they shook hands. She looked at Ginny, nodded, and squeezed Germaine's hand. Then she was gone.

"Now if the Old Man had a wife like that," he said, "he'd be governor."

"Or a fry cook," Ginny said sweetly.

He sat down and they laughed and started in on their salad bowls.

Old Dussault was stretched out on the davenport when they entered the house, his shoes off, the Sunday papers scattered around the floor. A dead pipe lay in the ash tray, an empty beer bottle stood on the coffee table. He stirred and opened his eyes as they watched.

"Ginny," he said. His eyes focused and he saw Germaine and sat up, clearing his throat and fishing for his shoes. "Germaine."

"Hello, Ed."

"I wasn't expecting company," he said. "I must have dozed off a little. Sit down, sit down."

Germaine sat in a fat, faded chair. Ginny remained standing.

"Something to drink," Dussault asked. "Whisky? Beer?"

"No thanks, Ed."

"Coffee then?"

"Well, that would be all right."

Ginny moved forward and picked up the pot along with the empty beer bottle.

She smiled at him and left.

Dussault finished lacing up his shoes and leaned forward, reaching his hand across the table.

Germaine took it and they shook hands.

"Nice to see you, Germaine."

"Nice to see you too."

Dussault waved his hands and then clasped them.

"I hope you had a nice evening."

"It was fine. We went down to the Smith Brothers Shanty."

"Good, good." He reached for his pipe and Germaine offered him a cigarette.

He took it and they watched each other as Germaine worked the Zippo.

"Ed," he said, "I want to marry Ginny. Is that all right with you?"

The old man blew out, exhaling through his nostrils.

"Germaine, you don't have to ask that. If it's all right with her, it's all right with me. And I can tell it's what she wants."

"It's okay with you?"

"It's okay with me," he said. "You know, you already

asked once about marrying her. When you were seventeen years old. You remember that?"

"I remember."

The old man nodded.

"Well, it was all right with me then and it's all right now. She waited for you a long time, Germaine. She's a good girl. College. Teacher. You know that."

"Yes," he said. "I know that."

Dussault worked his lips, seating his teeth.

"A woman should be married," he said. "And a man too. This is no life."

Germaine didn't say anything.

"I should have married again," Dussault said. "After her mother died. Then Ginny wouldn't have wasted so many years taking care of an old man in an old house. Well, that's the way it goes, I guess." He looked at Germaine earnestly, his jaw set.

"She's a good girl, Germaine. You probably heard things about her accident but she's a good girl. I wanted to die when she got crippled like that, but I'm to blame for that too. I kept too tight a rein on her when she was young. She wasn't wild or anything but when she got out I guess it was natural for her to kick up her heels. She needed a mother to raise her, tell her things her pa just don't know how to tell her. I wasn't much at raising her alone, Germaine. It's a wonder to me how she turned out to be such a fine woman."

"It's no wonder to me," Germaine said. "She's your daughter, Ed."

Ginny came in carrying a tray full of coffee cups and cookies.

"You going to get married in church?" Dussault's question was directed to no one in particular.

"No, not in church," Ginny said.

She set the tray down and took her father's hand.

"It doesn't make any difference," she said.

"No, I guess not," Dussault said. He held her hand. "Only I think you should talk it over with Father Joe." He looked at Germaine. "He shouldn't have to just hear about it from somebody. You understand, Germaine?"

"Sure," Germaine said. "It's all right. We'll go see him if you want."

Dussault nodded.

"I would like that," he said. "You know Father Joe. He would take it as a personal insult if you just left. It would be like running away."

"We'll go see him," Germaine said.

"Do you think it'll make him mad?" Ginny asked.

"No, I don't think it will make him mad," Germaine said, "I know damn well it will."

His mother was waiting up in the kitchen when he got home.

"You're going to marry Ginny, aren't you?"

"Maybe. You never can tell, Ma," he said.

"Oh, Germaine. I'm so happy. When are you going to see Father Joe?"

It was too long a story to go into tonight and he knew she would misunderstand. But he didn't intend to sit up the whole night arguing with her.

"Tomorrow," he said simply. "Tomorrow."

15

Germaine and Ginny went to see Father Joe the following afternoon.

"I wonder what he'll say," Ginny said. Germaine took her arm as they walked up to the rectory.

"I wonder what Roger will say when he gets home tonight."

"Are you going to tell him tonight?"

"I think," he said, "Mama will beat me to it."

The priest was affable as he opened the door.

"Well," he said, "two of my favorite parishioners."

He led them into the quiet, darkly varnished study. They seated themselves on the bulging mohair sofa and he asked them if they wanted some coffee.

"The housekeeper just made a pot before she left," he

said. "No? Well," he clapped his hands together, "what can I do for you?"

Ginny looked at Germaine uncertainly. He nodded.

"We're going to be married, Father."

The priest stared at her for a long time and then he smiled.

"Good. Good." He reached for Germaine's hand.

"Congratulations. Of course," he chuckled, "I'm not exactly surprised. I had a hunch you two might get together after all. Well," he slapped his knee, "this calls for a drink. Germaine, I think it might be fitting if we toasted the bride." He opened a cabinet door and pulled out a brandy decanter.

"Father," Germaine said, "maybe you should hear what the bride has to say first."

Ginny bit her lip.

"It won't be a church wedding, Father."

The priest turned to Germaine.

"Why not?"

"Well, Father," Germaine said, "I'm not really in the Church any more."

"Oh, bosh. Of course you are. A good Confession and you're all fixed up."

Germaine shook his head. "I'm not going to Confession."

The priest came back with the brandy and sat down. He spoke to Ginny, quietly.

"You knew this? You realize what this means? I can't marry you under those circumstances."

She nodded.

The priest's voice was a deep whisper. "And you would marry him anyway? Outside the Church?"

"Yes."

Father Joe set the decanter down on the coffee table.

"But you're *both Catholic*," he roared. "This is the damndest thing I ever heard of."

Germaine shrugged.

"It's a funny world, Father."

The priest unstopped the decanter and filled three glasses.

"I don't understand you, Germaine. Doesn't living in mortal sin bother you?"

Germaine didn't answer.

"Well," the priest repeated, "doesn't it bother you?"

"Father," Germaine said patiently, "we've been through this before. I believe in God but I don't believe the Catholic Church has an exclusive franchise on Him."

The priest turned sharply to Ginny.

"And what do you believe about the Church?"

She flushed.

"I love Germaine, Father. I just want to live with him."

"Answer my question," he demanded. "Would living in mortal sin bother you?"

"Yes," she said softly.

The priest looked at Germaine.

"And marrying outside the Church would be a mortal sin?"

"Yes," she said.

"Well," the priest said triumphantly. "Living in mortal sin would bother her. And if you died in that state, what would happen to you?"

Ginny's head was lowered now.

"What would happen?" the priest persisted.

Ginny's reply was barely audible. "I would go to hell," she said.

"Now, Virginia," the priest said, "is it worth it? A few years of sleeping with Germaine? And then the loss of your immortal soul?"

Ginny didn't answer.

Her hand was covering her eyes and her face was wet.

Germaine watched her closely. She was crying.

"Think about it, Virginia," the priest said. "Is it really worth it? Your immortal soul. And the souls of your children. Born in sin?"

She looked up slowly, her eyes red and glistening.

"I don't think God will punish me for being a little happy during my life, Father."

Germaine moved to Ginny and helped her to her feet. She buried her head in his shoulder.

"Well, Father," Germaine said, clasping the priest's hand, "we thank you for your advice and consideration. You must come see us sometime."

Then they were gone, and the priest watched them walking away. He looked down at three untouched brandies on the coffee table. Holy Mother Church had indeed fallen on lean days when Catholics could walk away from her with never a backward look. The powers of the flesh, he thought. He picked up one of the brandy glasses. Well. If ever a woman needed a man to love that woman was Ginny Dussault. He remembered her past confessions and wondered idly how the confessions of Roger LeMere would now be affected. Germaine would be kind to her, the priest knew. He sipped the brandy.

"Well," he said out loud, "they're *Your* rules, not mine. I just carry out Your orders."

He finished the brandy and picked up the second glass. Through the windows he could see the pickup truck pulling away. He reminded himself to read St. Malachi again. The old prophet fascinated him more and more. Only six more popes after Pius the XII, the Saint had prophesied. Only six more. Then what? The priest watched the truck vanish, and cradled his glass. Six more popes. And then what? He finished the drink, set it down, and picked up the last glass. He stood in the darkening rectory.

"And then what?" he said out loud.

It was dark when Germaine drove up to the proud old house on the fisherman's beach. The station wagon was parked in the garage, which meant that the Old Man and Roger were back. He pulled up behind it, turned off the ignition and rolled up the windows. He walked to the house slowly, letting the clean wind wash the tiredness out of him.

Roger was sitting with Mama at the table.

Germaine slid into a chair.

"Well," he asked, "how did it go in Madison?"

Roger was mopping up his plate with a slice of bread.

"Great," he said, without looking up. "How did it go in Two Rivers?"

"Where's Pa?"

"He's upstairs," Mama said. "Sleeping. I've never seen him so tired. Poor man. All that chasing around. Have you eaten, Germaine?"

He nodded.

"I ate in town, Mama."

She brought the coffeepot and sat down.

"Well," he asked, "what happened in Madison?"

Roger stuffed the bread into his mouth and licked his fingers.

"Nothin'," he said. "Ah, a lot of talk. But nothin' happened. And nothin's gonna happen, for at least a year. And maybe not even then."

"Did Pa get a chance to talk?"

"Yeah," Roger said. "Pa got a chance to talk. Everybody and his brother got a chance to talk. I never heard so many half-assed talkers in my life. The state claims we're to blame for takin' too many trout in the nets all these years. That's why the trout are down now."

Roger struck a farmer match and the sulphur smell filled the kitchen. He lit his cigarette and snapped the match in half.

"That's what the experts say," he reflected. "Now I'd call that pretty half-assed, wouldn't you?"

Mama poured the coffee.

"Your father said it was all a waste of time, Germaine. He said they were very polite but they had their minds made up."

"They weren't all that polite," Roger said. "One of the top guns at the Conservation Department, I forget his name, he told Pa it was the commercial fishermen's own damn fault for putting too much pressure on the trout. Now that's just crap."

"What about the lampreys?"

"Oh, they said there might be something in the lake. But not enough to affect the fishing. Besides they said there would be a natural balance that would control them. That conservation guy told Pa he wanted a control on the commercial fishermen. They want us to take fewer trout out of the lake so there'll be more trout in the lake and then they'll all multiply and that will solve our problem."

Germaine stirred his coffee. "Is there any chance they might be right after all?"

"In a pig's eye they're right. We'll all be out of business before they're right."

They sat there with their thoughts. Roger earnest and angry, Mama clutching a hand to her mouth.

"Well," Roger said finally, "we'd better go out and lift the nets tomorrow, okay?"

"Okay."

He ground out his cigarette and stood up.

"I wanna get into a nice hot tub and soak for an hour. My old butt is draggin'."

They stood facing each other and then Mama excused herself and left them.

"Mama was telling me," Roger said. "You and Ginny are gettin' married."

Germaine nodded.

Roger rubbed his nose and lowered his voice.

"I don't know how to say this but—well—you know I lipped off about her and well, talked pretty damn loose about her. But she is a good kid, Germaine. I mean, well, that's what I mean. She's a good kid." He looked into Germaine's face. "I guess she was always waitin' for you. You know what I mean."

Germaine nodded.

"I got thinking down in Madison," Roger went on. "And I figure, well, if you're both goin' back to Europe or somewhere and if we didn't see each other for a long time again, maybe never—well, I mean, we're still brothers and there's no hard feelings. About anything. Honest. Okay?"

He extended his hand and Germaine clasped it.

"No hard feelings," Germaine said. "I'd rather shake your hand than get hit with it."

Roger slapped him on the forearm.

"Well," he said, "I didn't have the guts to come right out and apologize, but you know what I mean." He squeezed Germaine's hand tightly and then he was gone up the stairs.

Mama came back as the door closed.

"It was all his own idea, Germaine. He told me he had to do it."

"He's a good boy, Mama. And I think he's growing up."

Mama shook her head.

"I thought I would never see the day. Now, what did Father Joe say about you and Ginny? Was he surprised?"

"Well," Germaine said with a glance at the clock. "Yes and no. You know Father Joe." He got out his cigarettes and the lighter; she leaned forward on her elbows.

16

The state wardens were waiting on the high skinny docks when Germaine swung the *Ione* into the harbor mouth. Then Roger came back and squeezed into the tight pilothouse.

"It makes a man mad to see them waiting," he said finally. Germaine nodded and stared out through the flat dirty glass.

Reuben looked at the men on the pier with the herring gulls rising around them as the *Ione* closed slowly and the barb-sharp stink of river smells came in from the flat water.

"What about the sturgeon?" Reuben asked. "Is that why they are waiting for us?"

"I don't think they know anything about the sturgeon,"

Roger said. "You tell your brothers to just unload as always. We are all right, understand? Don't even think about the sturgeon." The boy said yes and went down the deck.

The state men didn't move all the while the fish tug was mooring. None of the fishermen said anything and after the engine cut and coughed out, the only sounds left in Reuben's ears were the slivery gull screams and the boots of his brothers slopping around the hold, getting into position to take off the fish boxes. The wardens moved closer together and took out cigarettes and were talking low, watching the work. They all looked to be strangers to Reuben. Roger might know them, though, and he looked to the pilothouse. It was hard to see because the sun made a mirror out of the wheelhouse window and his brothers didn't come out right away. When they did Germaine walked over to him.

"Come on, Bébé," he said. "We better give the watchdogs something to watch."

Reuben and Germaine carried the fish box from the boat and onto the dock and set it down by the river wall of the gear shack next to the boxes already unloaded. As they walked back for another box, the state wardens moved to the boxes and stood to one side, smoking.

Roger came up the bleached boards holding the keys to the gear shack.

Germaine and Reuben hauled the very last fish box into shore and the state men shifted toward Roger and the big one in the middle turned and spoke.

"LeMere?" he asked.

Roger stopped.

"Yeah," he said.

"George LeMere," the warden said. "Is that you?"

"No, that's not me," Roger said. "That's our Old Man."

"Well, we want to see your catch," the warden said.

"It's all in the fish boxes," Roger said. "Packed up in the ice."

The wardens looked down at the wet boxes at their feet. The one who was doing all the talking addressed Roger again.

"You wouldn't have any undersized fish packed in the bottoms, would you?"

"No," Roger said, "I wouldn't have any undersized fish."

"That's what they all say," the warden said turning to the others, "it's the same every time." He turned back to Roger.

"All right," he said. "You might as well dump out the boxes."

"We're all legal," Roger said.

"You better be," the warden said. "We want to look at those fish boxes." He pointed to the boy. "All right. We can save the talking for some other time. You start dumping out those boxes now."

Reuben looked around at Roger and at Germaine and at the twins.

"It doesn't seem right to ask him to dump out the boxes," Roger said, "since he spent the whole damn morning filling them up."

"You do it then," the warden said.

"You go to hell," Roger said.

"What's your name?" the warden asked.

"LeMere," Roger said. "Roger LeMere. L E M E R E. And you can go to hell."

"You gonna dump these boxes or are we?"

"We're all legal," Roger said. "We don't have any small lake trout."

"That's what all you bastards say. All right, we'll find out." The three wardens bent and upturned every fish box and the dock exploded under the impact of chunked ice and skittering trout bodies. The pier looked like a slaughterhouse floor. The wardens poked among the gutted fish with their toes and measured with their eyes.

Germaine got out his pipe and began to pack it.

"Notice, my charming friend," Roger said to the big warden, "the scar holes on the trout. The lamprey eels are killing the trout. Why don't you pass a law against *them?*"

"We just want you to stick by the law you got," the big warden said.

They stood staring down at the fang-like holes in the trout bodies.

"You know where you can stick your law," Roger said.

The big warden's face rippled a little like a wind shift over a sand bar.

"LeMere," he said, "Roger LeMere." He was going to say more but instead he stopped and the smile came back.

"We're not looking for trouble, LeMere. We're only doing a job. You commercial fishermen overfished the lake trout. The state of Wisconsin passed a law to protect the lake trout and you bootleg and break that law and so the state of Wisconsin sends us here to make that law stick." The warden closed his eyes and he looked like a schoolboy reciting from memory. "If you got a grievance, take it to the legislature. We don't make the laws, LeMere. We just make them stick."

The warden stopped and slowly opened his eyes. "That's

how it stands, fisherman. You brought it on yourselves."

"Why don't they outlaw the lamprey eels?" Roger said. "That's what's killing the lake trout."

The warden's voice was very low when he finally spoke. "They say there's a lot of illegal sturgeon taken in nets up here too." He stared at Roger. "Don't make it too hard for yourself, fisherman." Then he turned and led the other state men off the dock and up the rickety bleached steps to street level.

The brothers started in to load up the loose fish in all the boxes and everybody began talking at once.

"We could clean up on them easy," Roger said. "We could beat the living Jesus out of them."

"They could put us all on the beach," Germaine said softly. "They could put the Old Man right out of business."

Roger spoke then and Reuben got a frightened feeling at the quiet voice.

"That big warden scare you, Germaine? Did he take the living guts right out of you?"

"You can't fight them," Germaine said. "They are the law and they could break the Old Man. That's what I meant. Only that."

They all went back to picking up the gutted trout and repacking them in the fish boxes.

Reuben had never been permitted to go along in the dory when they went out to the nets at night to lift an illegal sturgeon, and now a tingling chill moved over his back as he thought of this greatest of all sturgeon fish locked and trapped in the sunken pot net on the fish grounds.

"Can I go when you take him out? When you go for the sturgeon?"

"It's a man's work, Bébé," Germaine said.

"It is four men's work," Roger said. "This sturgeon is no perch fish, Bébé."

The brothers nodded.

"Please, Roger," Reuben pleaded. "I can help you."

"No," Roger said.

"Please, Roger. Please."

"No, Bébé, do not beg."

"I can help you."

"No."

"Please, Roger."

"Your turn will come."

"Please, Roger."

"Dammit," Roger bellowed, "no, Bébé! Now enough!"

Slowly they bent to their work and suddenly Reuben wanted to swear at them all and hit them and see them hurt and bleeding. He picked up a lake trout and flung it like a rock into Roger's face and it slopped loosely in his slickered lap.

"Goddamn you," he screamed. "Goddamn you! I am not a baby!"

And then he shook and cried and closed his eyes as tightly as he could. He wanted Roger to hit him as hard as he could and then he would be hurt and bleeding and then before he died he would forgive Roger everything and feel Roger's beard against his face. When Reuben opened his eyes Roger was not even looking at him.

"He goes," Roger said. "Bébé goes."

"In place of who?" Gabriel asked.

"In place of no one," Germaine said. "We make room for him."

Reuben crouched like a puppy and felt the tears on his face.

"What about the Old Man?" Germaine asked.

"He is not to know," Roger said. "Until later perhaps. Bébé," he continued, looking at the boy directly for the first time, "you will come with us after the sturgeon, but you will not tell a word to the Old Man at all. Do you understand? Not a word to Mama either!"

Reuben shook his head slowly yes. The chill began on his back again and though he tried to control it, his whole body shook a little bit even though the sun was like hot water on his body.

"Now," Roger said, "do not think about that any more."

Reuben almost shouted out the words as he asked his brothers the most important question of all.

"Are we going after the sturgeon *tonight*?"

"Tonight," Roger said and from his lap he picked up the trout thrown at him and gently lobbed it into the fish box.

"Now think of something else, Bébé. And say a few Hail Marys for the Old Man's great fish."

"They never say that in school . . . to pray for a fish," he said. "A fish is not like people."

"Why not?" Roger said. "People are like fish."

Reuben did not understand but Roger did not laugh and so he prayed to the Blessed Virgin for the great sturgeon.

"And what shall I pray for," Reuben said. "I mean, should I pray for something special for this fish?"

"Just pray that he has a good death," Germaine said. "That is all a great fish can want."

Reuben still did not understand, but his brothers all fell silent and so he was silent too, although his lips moved as they always did in school when he said his prayers to himself . . . half whispering and seeing the Blessed Virgin Mary wearing her blue robe and smiling, like his mother in the pictures of her when she was young.

Roger watched Reuben carefully and slowly wiped the fish-wet of the lake trout from his face.

At the supper table, the talk was all of the big sturgeon in the pot net nearly a mile out in the lake. The brothers spoke carefully of getting the fish out and Reuben nearly burst with the excitement of listening and knowing he would be helping them, yet not being able to talk about it in front of the Old Man and Mama. The booming of the surf outside sharpened his senses like barbed hooks and he could see the great six-foot body of the sturgeon rolling like some animal fenced in by the cable-like nets. He went to the kitchen window and stared out over the darkening lake. The Old Man reached out and rubbed his head as he went by to the living room for the pipe and tobacco.

Then he was aware of Mama and the laundry-starch smell of her holding him by the shoulders. He just stood there waiting for her to let him go.

"This is not a life for an honest man, Bébé." She was speaking as if to herself. "To sneak like a thief for the illegal sturgeon fish . . . and always the deep waters waiting. You must not bring a woman into this life, Bébé." Then she released him quickly and he followed her back to the table.

"There is a heavy swell running," Mama said loudly. "It is going to storm. I do not think that you can lift tonight."

"We can lift tonight, all right," Roger said, moving his cup for more coffee. "Or any night of the blessed week for that matter."

"Can you not wait for a quiet night?"

"What's to wait, Mama?" the Old Man said. "The state wardens are like mosquitoes on quiet nights. A little wind and a little sea running will hold them to the beach like flies."

"Yes? And what of this excitement for your heart? You all know what the doctor said."

"Mama," the Old Man said evenly, "you are making the excitement. We must get the fish out of there tonight or he tears up the nets and the whole rig comes out for repair."

Mama started to interrupt.

"Now, enough," the Old Man said raising his hand. "That fish is in our pot net and he comes out tonight."

No one said anything until Mama spoke.

"And what of the wardens? The wardens will be watching."

"We will get him out tonight," the Old Man said. "He is money in the bank."

Roger agreed. "We can peddle him in Milwaukee like nothing. Tail and all."

"*You* will get him out," Mama said angrily. "What do you mean *we*?"

"The boys and I will go for him tonight," the Old Man said firmly.

"The boys and you!" Mama turned, angry again. "Are you gone crazy in your old age? I will not let you leave this house. You will kill yourself with that fish. And what of the wardens? My God!"

"I will not die in jail," the Old Man said. "Not an old gull like me. They would have every fisherman an outlaw. What the hell. Is it against the law for a man to feed his family?"

No one said anything.

"A black, rough night," the Old Man said. "They won't be able to see their noses."

The brothers looked as if they wanted to do something for the Old Man.

"I think it will be all right tonight, Pa," Germaine said. "I do not think this will give us any trouble."

The Old Man started to argue with Germaine.

"This one last time," the Old Man said; "I wanted to go for one last great fish." He looked at his sons slowly. "It is something a man understands, I think."

Germaine nodded in agreement. "We would like you to come, Pa," he looked at Roger, "except that we would be crowded in the boat tonight."

"How do you mean crowded? There would just be the five of us," the Old Man said.

"There would be the *six* of us," Germaine corrected him. "Since this morning we have agreed that Reuben was to help us tonight."

"Bébé!" The Old Man's hand came crashing down on the table and everything rattled. "Bébé! I forbid it. A boy to go after that sturgeon? Germaine, you do not act wisely with your talk. Is this your doing?"

"This is all Bébé's doing," Roger said. "This morning he showed us he was a man. Now maybe he ought to do a man's work."

The Old Man relaxed his hold on the table and turned slowly to look at the boy.

"This is so, Bébé?"

"Yes, sir."

"And you are a man now? A man?"

Reuben looked directly into his father's eyes.

"Yes, sir," he said.

The Old Man stared round at the sons for a long time without speaking and then he pulled Bébé to him and slapped him on the buttocks.

"So then, your first great fish. For the Old Man this one, yes?"

Reuben told him yes.

"So Bébé will be no more Bébé. We are all men here now."

The brothers began to smile and Reuben thought the Old Man was going to stroke his head again but he didn't.

"What did he say?" the Old Man asked. "How did you know this manhood was upon him?"

Roger rubbed his nose.

"He threw a trout in my face."

The Old Man shook his head and punched Reuben's arm.

"You did not want to miss him at all, it seems."

The Old Man called for whisky glasses then and said that he wanted to drink once with his menfolk all together and although Mama didn't exactly smile she did what he asked.

"And bring a glass for Bébé also," the Old Man said. "This day he has a little something with his ginger ale."

The Old Man pulled the boy close again and he could hear his brothers laughing and the pounding of the Old Man's heart and, over all, the Lake Michigan surf boiling onto the beachlands beyond the dunes.

• • •

Reuben did not know if it was the excitement of actually starting for the pot nets or if it was the rolling water that dipped under the dory but when they were a half-mile out from shore, his mouth filled up with supper and the taste of whisky and he hung over the gunwales and was sick. The wind was blowing in straight off the lake and it carried cold spray into the back of his neck and he wanted to huddle under a thwart and fall asleep. It was completely dark without stars or moon and the wind and the waves moving sounded like a thousand waterfalls. Only the long, swinging yellow beam of Point Beach light seemed secure and not floating. They were jammed into the little dory like survivors on a raft and Reuben was afraid because they were thrown about so much and he couldn't see anything at all around them.

He reached his hand down over the gunwale and, as they dipped, the water swallowed up his hand and part of his jacket sleeve. He wiped his mouth and face clean.

Then he heard Germaine yelling in his ear. "How do you feel now?"

He said all right. "I was feeding the fish a little bit," he said.

Germaine slapped him on the leg.

"She is rough tonight," he said. He was still speaking but the wind was blowing away his words.

"What did you say?" Reuben yelled.

"I said we were almost there now."

"The hell you say," Roger shouted. He and Raphael were working the oars and they hadn't said anything at all until now. Roger was still talking but the boy couldn't hear and he yelled at Roger. Roger's voice came back slicing the wind like a knife.

"You were feeding the fish, hey?" There was laughter on the wind.

Reuben still felt very sick and was breathing in every time the dory went up and breathing out when it went down in the wave troughs. He was glad Germaine was not asking him anything so he would have to talk.

They just kept rising and falling and sliding and he tried hard not to think about anything that would bring back the sickness. He watched the Point Beach light swinging around and he counted one hundred thirty-nine revolutions and then he stopped counting. He watched the light so long it seemed to be getting closer and he got the feeling they were sliding stern first back onto the Old Man's beach.

Then Germaine was shading a flashlight in his hands and snapping it on and off and swinging it quickly. In the bending beam of the little light Reuben could see the forest of spile tops that poked out of the rolling waters like fence posts and the webby stiff glistening nets that strung out in great sprawling perimeters. They were in the fish grounds. Instinctively, his brothers had their position fixed and the light snapped out and they pulled for the lead side of the pot net—the side that could be loosened and lifted—the side to which they would moor while they brought up the net and the great sturgeon fish.

They made fast to two towering spiles with bow and stern lines and the water rolled through the nets and lifted and banged them into the spile sticks with a grinding, crushing sound.

"Keep your arms and hands inside," Germaine shouted. "She plays for keeps tonight."

The lead lines of the pot net were loosened from the spiles and they began the work of lifting the net by hand. As the sturgeon was free to swim around in the pot net, the plan was to raise the net under him, forcing him to the surface where he could be shot and hauled into the boat. The net was tarred stiff like iron cable and seemed to weigh tons. Germaine and Raphael were in the stern, Roger and Gabriel were up front. Reuben knew he was not much help to anybody.

"Your end," Roger would shout. "Your end, Germaine!"

"My end," Germaine would mutter, "my Royal Canadian end! All right, pull, Rafe. Put your back into it. Now, pull!" They pulled and pulled and together they rested and held their purchase and felt the current pulling against them below and then they pulled again. It seemed as if hours were going by every time the Point Beach light swung by and then the nets were swinging too and the spiles and their dory and the boy was convinced that the light was stationary and not moving and that he was swinging past the light like a stone on a string.

"Germaine," Roger was yelling, "the light! I think we have him up."

Reuben's pulse nearly pounded out of his temples. Germaine played a flashlight out over the pot net.

"There he is, Bébé! Look at the size of him."

The sturgeon rolled on the surface like some heavy log and sank out of sight. He was longer than a man. Germaine snapped out the light.

"Another ten feet," he yelled.

"Ten, all right," Roger answered.

"Another ten feet. And then this net will be under his belly. He has no place to go but up. Pull, pull!"

The ten feet of net came up slowly, like scrap iron. The net was taut, like a floor under the fish. The sturgeon had only a few feet of water and then the iron-cabled net.

"Now, Bébé," Roger said. He worked the net around the spiles somehow so it hung and then he switched on the flash and handed it to Bébé and loaded the rifle. "Keep the light on his head, Bébé. On his head."

The boy watched the glistening armored body as it twisted and rolled in the wash of water. He grabbed hold of a spile to steady the light and then Roger fired and Bébé bolted upright from the thwart. The fish was thrashing against the net like an animal against a cage. The tears were blinding the boy.

"Bébé, get down!" Roger was screaming. "Get down!"

Then the dory lifted as the water slid into them with that sickening slow rush and the boy toppled into the water. *The flashlight,* he thought. *The flashlight will get wet. The flashlight isn't waterproof*. That is what the boy was thinking and then the flashlight and everything else went out and there was warm water filling up his nose.

The next thing he knew, the flashlight was swinging around and around his head like a stone on a string. He tried to grab for it before it went to the bottom.

"How do you feel, Bébé?" Germaine's face was in front of him but upside down. Then the boy knew he was lying down between Germaine's knees and Germaine was behind him and bending over him.

"I fell in," he said.

"You were going to feed the fish again, eh?" Germaine pulled something around the boy's neck and he knew that it was Germaine's jacket.

"Hey," Germaine said, "Bébé's okay. He sends his love."

Roger and Raphael began talking at once.

"I feel very religious tonight," Roger said. "First we baptize him and then we wet-nurse him."

"I'm sorry I fell in," the boy said.

"She was rough tonight," Germaine said. "It could happen to anyone."

"That fish knew you meant business," Roger said. "When he saw you come into the pot net I think he could have died of fright."

"Where is the fish?" Reuben asked.

"We are all sitting on top of him, the big bastard!"

"If he was any bigger he could have this boat all to himself."

"Close your eyes now, Bébé. We will be on the beach in a little while now."

The boy watched the slickered wide backs of Roger and Raphael swing toward him and then away and then back again. He felt with his legs under the thwarts and he could feel the sturgeon fish. He remembered what the Old Man said about this great fish . . . *the oldest thing in these fresh waters. Before there was this world and even before that, there was this fish in these waters swimming . . . the skin like rocks all wrapped in steel . . . feeding, it must have fed on the bottoms where the beaches are now . . . always swimming, it must have moved along and against the currents for a million years without touching shores. Without touching shores. Without touching shores.*

They pulled for shore and the boy straddled the terrible stone body with his legs. *For a million years, where the beaches are now.*

He remembered what Germaine had told him that morning and he prayed that the great fish had a good death. He was very sleepy and warm and the boat was rocking not so much now and the wind was far away.

"Is Papa going to die?" he said out loud although he did not mean to ask it out loud. There was no answer and he began to think he had only said the question to himself after all.

"We are all going to die, Bébé," the answer came back.

And because of the being sleepy and the rocking and the faraway wind, he could not tell who it was that finally answered. He tried very hard to know who it was, but then he could not tell at all.

They carried the sturgeon up the beach in the dark and the boy held the door open as his brothers struggled the fish into the house and down into the fruit cellar. The Old Man came to watch in his slippers and the pipe dead in his mouth. They watched him without talking because they knew he was thinking and going to say something and they did not want to spoil it by speaking first.

"It is a great one, this fish," the Old Man said. "There will be no other like this one."

He turned and Germaine closed the fruit-cellar door and they followed the Old Man upstairs and into the kitchen.

Roger got out the bottle of brandy and poured the shots and handed the glasses around. The water from their slickers and the boots puddled on the floor and the boy felt the excitement of being a real part of this for the very first time. This was a ritual on the fisherman's beach, to drink a toast to the great illegal fish that were fought out of the nets the hard way. At night, with a big sea running and the pot nets lifted by hand and everything against the law.

Roger smiled and gave the boy mostly ginger ale and not much whisky but that did not change the boy's feeling at all. He felt the slime on his hands and saw it on the sides of the glass and thought of the great stone body in the basement. *The oldest thing in the fresh waters.*

"So then," the Old Man said, "how did it go, Bébé, your first great fish?"

The boy thought about being sick in the boat and falling into the pot net and the fear he had of the sturgeon.

"Good," he said. "It went good, Papa."

"That is the way," the Old Man said. "With me tonight it went hard. We waited, Mama and me, like two old women. She was wanting you back here with her and I was wanting myself out there with you." The Old Man sighed. "That is the way."

"Yes, sir," the boy said because he did not know what else to say.

"It is not so easy at night," the Old Man said. "It takes a good man at night in the small dory."

Germaine cleared his throat and motioned with his glass to the Old Man.

"Pa. You toast, Pa. This is your fish."

"No," the Old Man said. "No. This is not my fish but I toast this last time." He looked at the boy. "Bébé. For you. For your fish." He held up the heavy green glass. "You will see many great things from this water and on the beach."

He stopped and looked squarely at the boy. "Do not be afraid of them. To Bébé." He held out the glass.

"To Bébé," the brothers answered. The glasses clinked and the brothers watched Reuben's eyes and he sipped from the drink. Roger refilled the glasses with his bottle and told the Old Man how it was out on the water, leaving out only about the boy falling into the net.

"I have been thinking tonight," the Old Man said. "About those wardens."

"Those bastards," Roger said.

"That makes nothing," the Old Man said. "I have been thinking about how to change the law for the nets."

The brothers looked at each other and back at the Old Man. Reuben knew the look in their eyes was pity.

"I am not crazy," the Old Man said. "I will go to Madison."

"Pa," Roger said patiently, "you can't lobby against those bastards. Jesus, you tried that."

"I do not go to lobby," the Old Man said. "I will go to make the law of this land."

"You mean politics?"

"Even so. I will go as a state senator." The Old Man smiled. "You know how many friends I have with the lake-trout fishermen. Good. They will elect me and I will go. I will tell our story to the whole state. About these sea lampreys."

Roger finished pouring the whisky and the brothers looked at each other and shifted on their feet. No one said anything.

Germaine saw how the Old Man was full of color again. He was talking and using his hands as he did when the *Ione* was over the fish grounds and the work was fast and hard and plentiful and there was almost no time to think.

"Damned right," he said finally. "It is a good idea, Pa. The fishermen need you down there."

"Roger steps into my shoes," the Old Man said. "It is not so hard to be on the beach then."

"You're still a tough old gull, Pa," Roger said.

Then the thrashing noises came like crashing glass from the basement. The Old Man, because he was standing in front of it, was the first through the cellar door. Reuben did not know if it was a dream or he had fainted or was dead. When he followed them down, the Old Man had it all done. The white fruit cellar was horrible with broken glass and berry juice. The Old Man was straddling the sturgeon with his back to his sons and the hatchet for kindling raised over his head, flashing and falling, flashing and falling like the breakers on the beach. The sturgeon fish stopped its swimming motion on the concrete floor and shivered like a man in the cold.

Reuben closed his eyes and squeezed them tightly and prayed and when he opened his eyes again the Old Man was standing, leaning in the doorway, his mouth closed and breathing deeply through his nose. His bathrobe was flung with blood and smashed-down berries and juice and he looked past his sons and was watching Reuben closely. The slime from the hatchet dripped onto the concrete and then the hatchet dropped from his hand and the Old Man slumped and fell forward to the floor.

Reuben screamed and Germaine leaped to the Old Man and bent over. The boy closed his eyes. It was all a dream. A dream. Dear God. Sweet God.

He opened his eyes and Roger and Raphael were huddled around the Old Man and looking at each other. Reuben was afraid to ask the question because of what the answer would be.

"Call the doctor," he cried. "Call Dr. Coutre!"

Germaine shook his head. He ran his hand over the Old Man's face and wiped the blood away and closed the Old Man's eyes and smoothed his hair.

"It won't do any good, Bébé."

"The fish was dead!" Raphael said. "My God, the fish was dead!"

Roger looked up and his face was painful to watch.

"It's my fault. I should have shot him again."

They stared down at the Old Man and their faces were wet with slime and water. Still Reuben knew they were crying. The fish, the sturgeon, had killed the Old Man. He ran and slipped and bolted to the black fish body and kicked it and it slid heavily. Reuben kicked it again and again.

"God damn you," he cried. "God damn you!"

Then he felt his arms pinned and his feet lifted from the floor and he was staring into Germaine's wet bearded face.

"No, Bébé," Germaine was saying gently yet rapidly. "No, Bébé, no, no!"

Germaine held him tightly and off the floor. Then Reuben began to sob and Germaine led him to the basement steps and they sat down.

"We better get Ma," Roger said.

Germaine shook his head. "Not yet. We'll carry him upstairs."

Reuben blinked and blinked and blinked his eyes and finally there were no more tears to come and he stared at the two bodies on the basement floor and he huddled against Germaine.

"It's all right," Germaine said softly to him, stroking the boy's hair. "Everything will be all right, Bébé."

The boy stared and the tears began again. Then he heard his mother's voice calling down the stairs. He closed his eyes tightly and plunged his head into Germaine's lap and cried, for the last time, like a baby.

Epilogue

We will walk along this watershed. By the old beaches. We must stand watching into the sorrowing winds. The wood is into this sand from all the old hulls. Quietly they slip in among the fishheads. The spray blows above the beach like rain. We stand wetted with our remembering. The golden gulls swim the heights and are gone. At the sand bars every spring the water gains. Like dogfish the dunes lie in among the duck grass. The Fisherman's Beach sleeping in the open grave. From here they watched the fat full trout grounds.

Now, no more the four o'clock mornings. The stiff gas engines rolling beyond the bars. The water goes into the lighthouse rocks with a banging. Above this beach the sandpipers scratch. Below, the sandworms.

We stand staring at the fish birds blowing. In the waters beyond, the weeds string like anchor chains out of the sand-boils. The spile driver barge lies like a broken wall. The dead bolts hang in the holes like worms.

In the deep waters of the Great Inland Sea the lampreys go driving into the trout bodies like nails.